Reckless Liaisons

Reckless Liaisons

Kayleigh Jamison

Black Lyon Publishing, LLC

RECKLESS LIAISONS
Copyright © 2009 by MELINDA MCBETH

Our books may be ordered through your local bookstore or by visiting the publisher:

www.BlackLyonPublishing.com

Black Lyon Publishing, LLC
PO Box 567
Baker City, OR 97814

This is a work of fiction. All of the characters, names, events, organizations and conversations in this novel are either the products of the author's vivid imagination or are used in a fictitious way for the purposes of this story.

ISBN-10:   1-934912-13-1
ISBN-13:   978-1-934912-13-3
Library of Congress Control Number: 2008944232

Written, published and printed in
the United States of America.

Black Lyon Historical Romance

"For my sister, Kelly,
who is and always will be my best friend."

Chapter 1

*T*he horse's hooves beat a clamorous tattoo against the cobbled streets, stirring the low fog that had settled like a blanket. Julia dug her heels into the stallion's taut flesh, urging him faster still.

With a grunt and a sharp exhalation of breath, he picked up speed, mane tossing in the wind, droplets of water splashing in his wake.

She had no concern for the scandalous picture she painted, streaking through the outskirts of London on the giant black stallion, legs straddling either side of the beast as a man would ride. Haste had been far more important than modesty, and she hoped the cloak of night's darkness would hide the inconspicuous nature of her dress. Her maid had borrowed the trousers and plain linen shirt from one of the stable hands. Her hair had been pulled back in a simple tie at the nape of her neck, and now strands of it came free, wrapped around her arms in stringy tendrils.

A rush of exhilaration, relief, and gratitude passed through her as she finally broke free of the city, leaving the lights and the warmth behind in a blur. The countryside stretched out before her, and she slowed her mount to a walk, allowing the horse a chance to rest as much as she dared. She couldn't stop, not until she'd made it to her destination. She wouldn't be safe until she was there.

Time passed. Minutes? Hours? It was hard to tell. The rain stopped and started intermittently, the moon disappearing behind the clouds for longer and longer stretches. For the first time since her impromptu flight, she realized the folly of her decision. How was she to make it to her grandfather's estate, all the way in Scotland, when she hadn't a clue where she was? With no money, no change of clothes, and no sense of direction, she was certainly in over her head. She could hear her father's voice in her head. *This is just like you, Julia, to act so recklessly. You'll bring ruin to this family.*

But that was how terrified she'd been of her father's decision. Even now, lost somewhere on what she hoped was a road leading north with only an intermittent sliver of moon to guide her, she preferred her current predicament to how she should have spent her night—on the arm of her new fiancé, a man she feared and despised. Her stomach churned at the mere whisper of his name in her mind.

The Earl of Suffolk, despite his suave veneer and strikingly handsome visage, carried himself with an air of sinister cruelty, stained with a black reputation that even his newly acquired wealth and title could not wash away. The ton feared him, whispered of his exploits behind fluttering fans and tilted glasses. He was the only eligible bachelor on the market this season that didn't have endless hordes of young debutantes being shoved in his direction.

It wasn't that he was a rakehell—such indiscretions were easily forgiven by an earldom and a heavy purse. No, it was the rumor of violence and depravity that kept the ton away. Brothel girls beaten and bloody in his wake. Former mistresses so bruised they were unable to appear in public for weeks. Men who had crossed him found dead the slums, if ever found at all.

Then there was the young debutante who had taken her own life after he'd compromised her and refused to marry her. If you seek the devil, seek no farther than Thomas Howard, her aunt had said. And Julia's father, desperate to marry his only daughter to a wealthy man who could pay off his gambling debts, had sacrificed her without a second thought. The daughter of a Viscount, she wasn't the most sought-after deb of the season, and her father had been unwilling to leave his fate, and hers, to chance.

The moment her engagement had been announced, she'd begun formulating a plan. When the Earl had caught her alone in the parlor and murmured lascivious promises of how he planned to delight in robbing her of her innocence, she'd known she had to flee. And as he'd blithely informed her that he saw no need to wait until their wedding night to pass the time in her bed, all thoughts of a well planned escape had mutated into a desperate urge to get away as quickly as she could.

Her mother's father was a Scottish Duke with a large castle just outside Edinburgh. Since the death of her mother seven years before, her grandfather had begged to have Julia come to stay with him in Scotland. If she could just make it to him, he would help her. He would not allow her to be bartered and sold to an English rakehell, to suffer the same fate Julia's mother had. The Viscount had charmed her, seduced her, married her for her money to satisfy debts that, even then, were dangerously large. Once the money had run out, he'd cast her aside, sending her to live in his country estate, visiting only rarely. In truth, Julia had known very little of her father growing up. It was only when she reached marrying age that he had shown any interest, had brought her to London and had his sister begin grooming her for introduction to the ton.

A muffled noise startled her out of her reverie and Julia realized she was not to be alone much longer. The sound of hoof beats behind her indicated that whoever they were, there was more than one, and they were moving fast. Highwaymen? Her heart lurched with sudden fear. She hadn't even considered the possibility of being accosted on the road. She attempted to calm her racing heart by reasoning with herself. Perhaps it was simply another desperate traveler such as herself.

Or perhaps it's your fiancé, her nearly hysterical mind screamed. It was no doubt well past the time, now, when she had been expected at Lady Winterton's soirée. The Earl had promised to do many things to her this evening, and most of them could be accomplished just as easily here, if not more so.

Thinking quickly, she steered her mount off the road and into the dense covering of the forest just as the moon slid behind the clouds, leaving her cloaked in complete darkness. She slowed the horse to a walk, acutely aware of the crunch of leaves beneath its hooves, and for the first time that night, found herself grateful for the rain as it muffled the noise of her movement.

The tree branch caught her unaware, slamming against the side of her head with a force that jarred her teeth. With a moan she slumped forward against the stallion, and succumbed to unconsciousness.

•

Sebastian Cade had seen many things in his two and thirty years. A massive black stallion trotting across the gardens of his estate with an unconscious figure slung across its back was not something he'd ever expected to witness.

Sitting behind the large oak desk in his study, sipping brandy and attempting to chase away the headache that had formed after a seemingly endless day of reviewing accounts and answering correspondence, he had glanced up at the rush of movement in his peripheral vision, highlighted by the light pouring from the kitchen on the opposite side of the manor.

He shook his head and looked a second time, expecting the strange vision to have disappeared. But no, there it was again. The horse slowed, lowered his head, and began to nibble with enthusiasm on the perfectly manicured bushes hedging the northernmost garden path. The rider, who had been slumped against the animal's wide neck, slid forward at the loss of support and toppled, face first, unceremoniously to the ground. Though dressed as a man, he deduced the rider was female from the tangled mass of long black hair, blended almost seamlessly with the nighttime darkness. Her mount seemed unconcerned—after a brief shake of its head in her direction, he returned to his grazing.

"Bloody hell," Sebastian muttered, rising to his feet and moving to the door of his study. He supposed the situation required investigation. He was exhausted, and in a rather foul mood after seeing how much money his younger brother had spent on gambling last month, but he couldn't very well leave a comatose girl sprawled in the midst of his roses.

"Milord." One of the maids met him in the hall. "Yer not going to believe this."

"There's a girl in my garden."

"Aye, milord. Did ye see 'er too, then? I'd stepped out o' the kitchen t' fetch some wood an' there she was. We couldn't find William, so Mrs. Holland said to fetch ye posthaste."

"Tell Mrs. Holland not to fret. I'm going to investigate."

"She also said to tell ye to be careful, yer Grace." The young girl handed him her lantern with a coy smile.

He grinned in spite of himself, rubbed a hand across his face, and took the lantern. His scar throbbed, as it often did when he was frustrated.

"Do tell Mrs. Holland that I can take care of a small slip of a girl perfectly fine, especially one who is unconscious."

The older woman who served as his head of household had been his nurse maid as a child, and was the closest he'd had to a mother growing up, his own having died giving birth to Sebastian's brother. She'd been wildly protective of him in his youth and little had changed now about her opinion of his ability to care for himself.

With a final nod to the serving girl, he turned and headed for the back door of the manor, then out into the gardens and toward the crumpled heap barely visible in the milky blackness. The black stallion lifted its head and snorted at his approach. It was an impressive animal—ridiculously large for such a small girl, clearly bred for racing. He'd have it cared for as soon as he saw to its rider.

"Well," Sebastian murmured, crouching down to brush thick black hair from the girl's—no, *woman's* face, "this makes things interesting."

She was indeed a woman, he realized as he set down the lantern. Gripping her shoulders, he gently turned her onto her back and a pair of deliciously full breasts swayed into view beneath the torn fragments of her shirt, snared by the rose bush's thorns. The rest of her figure was slender and girlish but the swell of enticing porcelain flesh that rose and fell with each ragged unsteady breath proved his damsel in distress was certainly not a child. Her clothing was crude, simple tan breeches and the now soiled, torn shirt, but on her feet were dainty women's slippers embroidered with green and gold.

It was almost humorous and had the circumstances been different he surely would have laughed. Her skin was pale and flawless, not the tone or texture of a servant or peasant girl. What the devil was a woman such as her doing face down in his garden dressed as a stable hand, let alone riding unaccompanied across the English countryside?

His eyes came to rest on her face, tilted to the side and resting against one slender shoulder. Fine, sculpted brows arched above eyes protected by lashes so long and full they brushed the apples of her cheeks in a graceful fan. He wondered what color her eyes were, and hoped, irrationally, they would be blue. High cheekbones and a tiny button nose gave way to a full pouty mouth and small chin that lent her face a heart-like shape. Turning her chin, he surveyed the left side of her face, and discovered the source of her unconsciousness. A vivid, purple bruise marred her pale skin, just above her left temple, and a jagged cut had leaked blood down her cheek, now crusted to a dull brown.

Skimming his hands along her form, Sebastian performed a cursory check for broken bones and was relieved to find none. He stood and lifted her into his arms, surprised at how light she felt cradled against his chest.

Mrs. Holland waited for him at the door, worrying her bottom lip and wringing her hands together.

"I need water and bandages," he ordered. "And clothes.

I believe my sister has some nightgowns in her old room. Someone locate my wayward valet and have him tend to the horse."

"Shall I send for the doctor, your Grace?"

"Not yet." With a shake of his head he started for the back staircase. "Help me tend to the wound, and then we'll decide how bad it is."

"Who is she?"

Sebastian paused and again shook his head, glancing down at the bundle in his arms. In the warm light of the kitchen she looked even more beautiful than his initial assessment had deduced, lips slightly parted, the ugly mess on the left side of her face the only indication something was out of sorts. Her chest rose and fell in a gentle rhythm, drawing his attention lower, back to her breasts once more. An angel? He bit back a laugh. Where had such an absurd thought come from? It reminded him of the things he'd once said to— *Don't*. "I've no idea."

He continued up the stairs to the sounds of Mrs. Holland scurrying about the kitchen gathering the items he'd requested. Carrying the girl down to the far end of the hallway, he shouldered open the last door on the right and moved to the large canopy bed that stood against the far wall.

He set her down as gingerly as possible, while the young maid bustled in behind him, lighting candles in his wake. The woman let out a tiny moan and stirred. One eye fluttered open briefly before drifting closed again.

"It's alright," he heard himself whisper. "You're safe."

He'd been right. Her eyes were blue.

Chapter Two

The first sensation Julia registered as she swam toward consciousness was pain. A dull, throbbing ache began at her head and pulsed its way down her body. She groaned and forced her eyes open, willing them into focus. One hand reached up to probe at her forehead and found it wrapped in several loops of cloth.

She didn't recognize her surroundings, but they were refined and tasteful, not the furnishings of an inn or country house. The bed was large with a polished cherry headboard and canopy overhead, the carved frame draped in lace and heavy fabrics. The entire room was coordinated in feminine shades of purples, creams and blues.

Sunlight peeked in through curtained windows, and beneath them sat a small breakfast table and chairs. In the opposite corner was an armchair covered in blue brocade. Across from the bed was a yawning fireplace, to the right of which stood a large armoire and a screened area for bathing to the left of it. A simple but elegant chair molding divided the walls, with cherry paneling on the lower half. The beauty of the room, though, was overshadowed by the uneasiness she felt in the unfamiliar setting.

What had happened?

She remembered arguing with her father. Over her betrothal. She'd taken his horse and … There had been men on the road… Oh, God! He'd found her. She was in his house! She bolted from the bed, ignoring the shards of agony lancing through her skull.

She was wearing an ankle-length night gown and nothing else. Where were her clothes? A frantic glance around the room revealed nothing. She limped to the armoire and threw open the doors, sifting through the contents—gowns, at least a dozen, all richly made but out of date. At the very back she spied a robe and yanked it from the hook, throwing it across her shoulders. It would have to do.

Julia crept to the door and flung it open, half expecting it to be locked. Peeking out into the corridor she saw that it was empty and began to make her way down the long hall, one hand braced against the chair railing for support. Her vision was blurry, her head spinning, lungs burning from exertion. She paused and caught her breath. Just a few more steps to the stairs. With any luck, she'd find herself in the front hall, and make it out the door before being spotted. If she could just get to the stables, get to a horse, she'd be free again.

"Miss!"

Julia let out a startled yelp and began to move again, twisting her head just long enough to identify a girl behind her looking as shocked to see her as she was to be seen.

The young maid ran to her, slipping an arm around her waist. "Ye mustn't be out o' bed!"

"Help me," Julia rasped.

"Ye've taken a nasty knock to the 'ead, ma'am."

"I have to get away. Lord Thomas will—"

"I don't know no Lord Thomas, Miss," the girl replied in a cockneyed accent, struggling to keep them both upright.

"I'm not … in his house?"

"No, ma'am." She gave Julia's arm a comforting pat, then lifted her head and shouted, "Mrs. Holland! Come quick!"

Out of the corner of her vision, Julia saw another figure approaching from the right. An older woman with a wide girth and slightly stooped posture rushed over and supported her from the other side.

"Come now, dear, you must lie back down," she cooed,

guiding Julia back to the chamber.

"No," Julia moaned. "No, I have to go."

"Hush. You're safe here." The pair were gentle but firm as they set her into bed once more.

Despite her urge to flee, she found she lacked the strength and allowed the two women to tuck her under the covers again. "Where am I?" she asked, groggily rubbing a hand across her face with a grimace. Already she felt better. With the strain off her feet her head began to clear some.

"Foxwaith Manor."

Foxwaith. Why did it sound familiar? "Who is master here?"

"His Grace the Duke of Rutland." With a pat on Julia's hand, the older woman shuffled to the door, the younger just on her heels.

Rutland? Dear Lord! She'd been introduced to the man's younger brother just last week at Lady Anders' dinner party. Lord Cade had been devilishly handsome, with an equally devilish reputation. He'd charmed her aunt to near distraction and the poor old woman had been fanning herself vigorously to hide her blush by the time he'd left their company.

It was said he would inherit the duchy when his brother passed, the current duke being either disfigured, or sickly, or both. Rutland was a bit of a mystery to the ton, since he never appeared in their midst, neither accepting nor issuing invitations. These theories about his health were according to Aunt Margaret, who had it on good authority from Lady Winterton, who'd heard from Lady Marbury, who'd happened upon a conversation between Lady Anders and Miss Williams —Julia shook her head as she attempted to mentally catalogue all the gossip she'd heard in the month since her debut. All she knew for certain was that Rutland's name was uttered with almost as much fear as Suffolk's.

Moments later she heard voices in the hall.

"She's awake, milord."

"How is she?" A deep baritone, the sound was mildly

intimidating.

"Confused and frightened."

"I'd just brought in some tea for her," the younger girl cut in, "and was on my way back to the kitchen when she tried to run downstairs."

"Did she give a name?"

"No, milord."

The conversation continued, but the trio lowered their voices, and Julia was unable to decipher anything. There was the rumble of the Duke's voice, followed by a shrill protest by the old housekeeper. A derisive comment, and another vehement return. They seemed to be arguing over something, and Julia guessed it had to do with her.

She'd nearly drifted back to sleep when the tap of boot steps outside the door roused her back to consciousness. It was a sure, steady sound—a man's stride. She tensed and drew the covers up to her chin. The door swung open, and the Duke of Rutland stepped inside, stopping several paces from the bed.

Julia focused her gaze on the man's lower half, which turned out to be a mistake. Black Hessians polished to a glossy sheen gave way to tan-colored breeches that sculpted muscular, strong legs, the ridges of his thighs outlined by the soft fabric in a most flattering way. No disfigurement there. She trailed her gaze up past his waist to browse the wide expanse of a broad chest, covered by a clean linen shirt. He was without a jacket or cravat, and the high collar of his shirt lay open, revealing an enticing curve of muscle and a smattering of wiry curls. She found herself transfixed.

He cleared his throat and her eyes snapped up. Embarrassed at having been caught staring so openly, she momentarily forgot her fear … and discovered it entirely unfounded in the first place.

Save a faded scar running the length of his cheek from right ear to chin, the man was flawless. He had a square, defined jaw with a slightly cleft chin, flanked by long sideburns that ended just below his ears. His nose was regal and aquiline, but slightly crooked, apparently broken some time in the past, set above lips that were, at the moment, drawn into a thin line that was almost a scowl and nearly a grimace. His bottom lip was slightly fuller than the top. Dirty blond hair curled loosely around his shoulders, mussed as if he'd just run his hand through it. One thick lock fell over his forehead and obscured intense, dark green eyes.

He was even more handsome than his younger brother, if such a thing were possible, and gave off an air of focus and seriousness, wholly opposite Lord Cade's playful flirting. She wondered when he'd last smiled, and guessed it had been a long time. Having cataloged each of his features separately, Julia took in his face as a whole, trying to gauge his mood.

Rutland's expression showed a mixture of annoyance and satisfaction. It rattled her, and in an attempt to break the tension she said the first thing that came to mind.

"You are not deformed at all," she blurted, feeling her face flush before she'd even finished the sentence.

He smirked and those gorgeous eyes flashed with amusement. "Is that the latest rumor, then?"

"I … Well, I mean …" Julia trailed off, unable to come up with a suitable denial.

"Would you care for tea?"

The sudden shift in the conversation, and the fluid manner in which he'd done it, threw her off balance once again. She nodded.

"I trust you are feeling better?" he asked as he poured two cups of tea from the side table, splashing a drop of brandy into one before carrying the other to her and setting it in her upturned hands. Then he settled himself into the reading chair in the corner of the room. Half in shadow, half in light, the planes of his face were slightly distorted as he watched her with sharp eyes that gleamed in the concealing darkness.

"Yes, your Grace. You have been overly generous in your hospitality. You certainly did not have to provide me with shelter, let alone dress and food."

"Miss, it's not every day—or in fact any day save the last, that a young woman gets dumped unconscious in my garden." She dropped her gaze. "I had little choice but to assist you."

Julia felt her blush spread. "I suppose I was a bit of a sight, wasn't I?"

"Mm," he gave a noncommittal mumble, and lifted his cup to his lips with such casual ease that she was wholly unprepared for his sudden bark of laughter. He set his cup back down untested, shook his head, and laughed again. "You were," he choked out before lowering his head, shoulders shaking in mirth.

"It's not so funny as all that, your Grace!" she protested, but within moments she was giggling herself. Lord, what a fool she must have looked. And after the pain, anger, and frustration of the last few days, it felt good to laugh, so she did.

Then she realized he wasn't laughing any longer. He watched her instead, and the intensity of his expression sobered her instantly. Again his lips were drawn together in a tight, firm line. It was a no-nonsense look, the look of a man who was accustomed to giving orders, and having them obeyed. She sensed that he hadn't intended to laugh, to show any emotion at all. As if he didn't already think her daft, which he surely did, here she was giggling like a foxed lightskirt!

"What is your name?"

"I … don't remember," she replied, but the lie did not flow smoothly. These shifts in mood were unnerving, she couldn't quite get the hang of the conversation no matter how hard she tried.

"And I … don't believe you," he countered.

"I hit my head on a branch, and such a blow can cause memory loss, or so they say," she shot back.

"True enough, but if that is the case, how do you remember where you hit your head?"

"Perhaps I guessed!" Julia all but shouted in her frustration.

He graced her with a laconic smile. "Perhaps you are

guessing now."

"As to what?" His grin was infuriating—and completely distracting. How could she be expected to concoct a successful lie when her brain refused to concentrate on anything save how soft his lips looked? She had never been kissed. She wondered what it would feel like. He had such a wonderful looking mouth.

"My intelligence, madam. I regret to inform you it is higher than you had hoped."

•

Sebastian sat across from his mysterious charge and did his best to hide his discomfort, as much as she displayed hers. Her eyes were even more stunning now that he'd had a chance to study them—a glacial, clear blue. They alternately widened and narrowed based upon the bizarre flow of the conversation. It wasn't his intention to be intimidating, but it had been some time since he'd had a normal, polite conversation with anyone.

He was finding the effort of it rather tiresome. In addition, he was distracted by the way she held the coverlet to her chin in a vice-like grip, apparently oblivious to the fact that he had been the one to carry her to the bed in the first place. He was already keenly aware of how supple and enticing she was under the mound of thick blankets.

Her mannerisms, though somewhat blunt, smacked of ton breeding. A seasoned (and in some ways reformed) rakehell, Sebastian could smell a debutante a mile away, and typically ensured they came no closer than that. Who she was, precisely, he had no idea. He hadn't set foot within London's limits in over five years, not since his father had taken ill and summoned him home to Lincolnshire, a request he'd been only too eager to obey since he would have grasped at any excuse to leave the season after what had happened.

The old Duke had died a few short months later, and Sebastian had steadfastly refused to return to London. He had no desire, he expressed, to be chased about by greedy, moon-eyed young debutantes with delusions of becoming a Duchess. His brother and sister, who visited him from time to time in his self-imposed reclusion, knew there was a deeper reason he shied away, but thankfully kept the subject out of conversation.

"Did you start the rumors yourself?" she asked, seeming to read his mind and startling him out of his reverie.

"What?"

"The rumors about you, you started them yourself, didn't you?"

"Why would I do a thing like that?" he snorted, but avoided her direct stare. Those luring eyes of hers made it difficult to lie, particularly when fixed on him in such an unswerving manner. The rumors had, in fact, been his own doing, and he was rather proud of their effect thus far. Since starting their circulation he hadn't received a single invitation or missive from anyone save his relatives.

"It's an effective way to keep oneself off the marriage mart."

"There are less extreme ways of doing that."

She shook her head and took a sip of tea. "Not for a duke."

"No?"

"A greedy mother or desperate father is willing to overlook a multitude of sins when the potential groom is titled, my lord," she intoned with a hint of bitterness. He had the impression she spoke from personal experience. "In fact, I imagine that not even a disfigurement would keep them away, and it's only the rumor of your impending demise that has given you your solitude. A duke can very nearly get away with murder."

Sebastian couldn't help but flinch at her last comment, quickly lifting his cup and taking a sip to hide his expression. Damn it, she was perceptive. Or perhaps, he was simply that transparent. None of the people he surrounded himself with ever dared confront him about his stubbornness; those who had, he now avoided. He was particular in his company, choosing only those who wouldn't force him to talk about things he didn't like to discuss. Already, this small slip of a girl was breaking past his carefully constructed defenses. How unfair it was of her to do so, when she was hiding secrets of her own. Ah, but that was is, wasn't it? So long as they were talking about him, they weren't discussing her. He decided to switch tactics.

"I'm guessing," he said finally, "that you still don't feel inclined to tell me your name."

"No, I don't," she replied, chin lifting in haughty defiance.

"Well then, I have no choice but to escort you to London and put out inquiries. I'm certain a missing young woman hasn't gone unnoticed or unmentioned. Someone will assist me in returning you to wherever it is you belong." He raised an eyebrow and fixed her with what his brother called his "ducal stare," waiting for her to take the bait. He'd rather ride straight to hell than into London, but she didn't know that.

"You can't!" she exclaimed, eyes going wide with fear. Her hands fisted in the bed sheet and she drew it up over her trembling chin. The color drained from her cheeks so rapidly that he felt a pang of guilt for being so harsh. He had a similar, internal reaction to the city himself. But finally, he had some information. She was terrified of London.

"For all I know, you are a fugitive hiding in my house. If you will not tell me your identity, I'll have to discover it by other means."

"Julia." She sighed in defeat.

"Now we're making progress," he smiled. "Tell me, Lady Julia, why you are so afraid of London."

"I'm not afraid. I just need to get to Edinburgh. If you would be so kind as to tell me the way, I will take my horse and leave, and not trouble you any further." That edge of defiance had crept back into her voice, that stubbornness that he was growing to despise and find endearing at the same time.

Sebastian snorted. He was a rake and a rogue and occasionally a bastard, but he wasn't a fiend. "Send you alone across the border? I think not. Tell me what you are running from."

"Nothing."

"I doubt it was nothing that propelled you out into the night dressed as a man on a horse three times too big for you."

"Maybe I was going for a ride and my horse got away from me. Maybe my outfit is the latest fashion!"

He glared at her. Little hoyden. "You're trying my patience."

"And you're trying mine," she shot back.

"Perhaps I can help with whatever trouble you are in," he sighed.

"You can't. Please, I wish to rest some, my head ..." Julia grimaced, and he felt another pang of guilt. Whoever she was, it was clear she wasn't going anywhere until she was recovered anyway. He didn't really believe her a criminal fugitive, she struck him simply as a very stubborn, very frightened young woman.

"Then I'll leave you be. I'll send Mrs. Holland up in a bit so that you may have a bath and some supper." Sebastian stood. "But I do expect you to tell me eventually."

He'd made it to the door when she spoke, voice barely above a whisper. "My lord?"

"Yes?" He threw a glance over his shoulder and saw that her eyes were bright with tears.

"If I had stayed in London, he would have harmed me. If he finds me now, I am certain he will kill me."

"So long as you are in my home, you are safe. You have my word." With a perfunctory nod, he left, letting the door click shut behind him.

He stopped in the kitchen and spoke briefly to his housekeeper before locking himself in the sanctity of his study, pouring himself a brandy and sinking into the chair by the fireplace with an exhausted sigh. Last night, he had stayed up till near dawn watching over Julia. Mrs. Holland, ever careful of propriety, had shooed him out of the room to change the girl's clothes, and only allowed him back in when she was safely tucked under the covers. He'd spent most of the night in the chair by her bedside, watching her sleep. She hadn't been in any danger, really, no fever, and the cut on her head hadn't looked nearly as bad once cleaned and bandaged. But he'd wanted to stay with her, for some inexplicable reason. In case she opened those blue eyes of hers again. In case she needed comforting.

She had looked small and fragile in the massive wooden bed, even more so than when he'd found her in the roses. Her skin was like porcelain, the contrast created by the onyx shade of her hair, so black it appeared almost blue as it framed her face had added a surreal quality to the entire tableau. A few times, she had moaned in her sleep, tossing her head against the pillow and he'd fought the urge to comfort her by gathering her against his chest and holding her close.

Sebastian tried to put a halt to his wayward thoughts. He knew all too well what trouble they would cause. Women, on the whole, were nothing but a headache; even his own sister, though she meant well, tried his patience frequently. He'd remained almost entirely celibate over the last five years, save one indiscretion when he'd been in his cups at a nearby tavern and the serving girl had done everything in her power to lure him into bed.

It was part of the reason why Julia unnerved him so. She was beautiful and enticing, innocent and stubborn. Her eyes were frustratingly expressive, he could read every emotion in those deep blue depths. One moment she was shooting fire at him, the next looking at him like she wanted him to seduce her. And damn it all to hell if part of him didn't want to do exactly that. Five years of solitude were taking a toll, even if he knew in his head that he deserved a hundred more. His body seemed to think otherwise. If he wasn't so bloody attracted to her, this would be a far easier situation to deal with.

Lighting up a cheroot, he inhaled and thought back to their conversation, mulling over her words. She was terrified of someone. A man. A lover? She seemed too innocent to be someone's mistress.

Yes, and you thought that once before, didn't you?

He needed to discover more about her and her situation. If she was indeed in danger, he could keep her safe. He scribbled a quick note to his brother, requesting his presence at Foxwaith. Alex was well-connected in London society despite his reputation as a rake, thanks to the expectation that he would inherit Sebastian's title in the near future. If Julia had been in London, chances were good his brother would recognize her.

It wasn't much of a plan, but it would do for the moment. Perhaps he'd be able to gain her trust in the days it would take for Alex to arrive. Or perhaps it was better to stay away from her entirely. The fact that he wanted her to trust him was unnerving. It seemed the carefully constructed wall he'd built around himself had some cracks, after all.

•

Julia spent the next few days in bed for the most part. The first, she could barely sit up without her head spinning and her stomach churning. Under the watchful eye of Mrs. Holland, who brought her a myriad of broths and sandwiches and doted on her like a child, she felt a marked improvement, and by the second day she was able to move about the room unaided, sitting at the small breakfast table to take her meals, and sitting by the fireplace with a bit of embroidery the housekeeper had provided.

The older woman was quite friendly and entertaining, and Julia grew fond of her. She was much like Julia's childhood governess had been, and seemed to possess a great deal of patience when it came to Lord Rutland. He did not come to visit her again, but from time to time she would hear him bellowing for the servants from somewhere in the house. While the younger maid, Elizabeth, would immediately go into a frenzy at the sound of his yelling, Mrs. Holland merely rolled her eyes and continued with whatever task she'd been about, not going to his aid until she'd finished it.

"It's partly my fault he's so surly," she'd commented. "He

lost his mother young, so I spoiled him. But before I leave this world, I'll rid him of it if it's the last thing I do."

By the fourth day, Julia was terribly bored. Truth be told, she despised needlework, in part because she was awful at it. Her finger had been pricked so many times it throbbed worse than her head, and she'd only made the attempt because she'd had nothing better to do. She was curious about the estate and couldn't wait to see more of it. The windows of her room overlooked the back of the property, with a sprawling maze of gardens and pristine, groomed green lawn beyond, flanked by a neat line of trees.

The stables were behind the house, to the right of the gardens. She could see the left side of the house—an L-shaped structure made of grey stone, three stories high with a square turret at the end; she assumed there was one on her side as well. She wondered how many servants were required to maintain the property, and if anyone other than the Duke was in residence. No wonder he was ornery, living in such a large space all alone.

After breaking her fast and bathing, she perused the armoire for something suitable to wear. The gowns belonged to Rutland's sister, Catherine, and were several years out of style, but Mrs. Holland had said Julia was welcome to them. Catherine preferred to stay in London and had no use for them.

Julia selected a powder blue morning gown with a scooped neck, short bell sleeves, and an empire waist, all trimmed in white lace. It wasn't a perfect fit. The Duke's sister shared some of his height and slim build so the dress dragged on the floor a bit. Julia's breasts were packed tightly into the bodice in such a way that she feared they'd spill out with one false move. But, it was better than nothing.

Spying a plain white shawl toward the back of the wardrobe she wrapped it about her shoulders, covering herself as best she could. She pulled her hair into a loose chignon, piling the raven locks on top of her head in a haphazard effort to tame the unruly mass, which never seemed to curl where she wanted. Aunt Margaret would have a fit, she thought as she examined herself in the mirror. Then again, the woman would faint dead away if she ever learned Julia had ridden through London dressed as a stable boy.

The shoes, she discovered, did not fit at all and so she padded out of the room barefoot, moving down the hall to explore Foxwaith Manor. The doors on this floor were all closed—likely bedrooms or store rooms, so she moved on until she reached the wide, curved staircase.

Once in the foyer, she surveyed her surroundings. The setting was warm and inviting, the walls covered in rich mahogany paneling, the parquet floor a slightly lighter shade. Silver sconces lined the walls, bathing the entire space in soft yellow light. A long table sat against one wall with a vase and ornate candelabra. A large grandfather clock perched against the other wall, ticking away the minutes with measured patience. One hallway branched off to the left, another to the right. Two doors flanked each hall, three were open. She guessed that the closed room was the Duke's office, and wondered if he was inside. Did he scowl as much when he was alone as he had in her presence? There was no denying he was handsome, almost unnaturally so, but it had been his eyes that had captivated her. He seemed so … lost. She couldn't help but wonder what had made him withdraw from society, going so far as to spread rumors to keep people away.

Julia wandered from room to room, running her fingers across the carved tops of the chairs in the dining room, set around a long, wide table, tracing the marble mantle in the front parlor, decorated in soft yellows and blues. Each room was immaculately decorated, meticulously cleaned. Rutland seemed to enjoy order, each accessory in its proper place. Fresh flowers brightened the rooms, which struck her as strange in a house that never saw company.

As soon as she entered the library, she knew it would be her favorite room in the house. It was as large as the ballroom, and the walls were lined floor to ceiling with bookcases, each filled to capacity. A metal staircase in the southeast corner of the room spiraled up to a balcony that edged the perimeter of the room, giving the space two floors, while keeping it open at the same time.

She'd never seen so many books in her life. Her father had thought it important to provide Julia with an education, but as she'd grown to maturity had frowned upon her bluestocking tendencies. When his debts had begun to get out of control, the family's collection of books had been the first thing to go. Though she'd managed to hide a few of her favorite volumes under her bed, she'd mourned the loss of the library, and had longed for a day when she could see its return.

Abandoning her cumbersome shawl on a red velvet chaise, she explored the room, moving counter clockwise from the door. The books were loosely organized based upon subject matter, starting with the sciences—biology, chemistry, medicine—and then moving on to philosophy, history, and religion, followed by fictitious works. She paused at the section dedicated to the classics, running a finger down the spine of each title as she read it. All the books she loved were here, every single one. Plucking one from the shelves, she fanned through the pages, eyeing the ink drawings that accompanied Homer's *Iliad*.

"You've found my favorite room," a voice sounded behind her, reverberating in the large space.

She whirled around to find the Duke in the doorway, one broad shoulder leaning against the frame. He wore tan breeches and polished black Hessians, much as he had the day she'd first seen him. This time his white blouse was partially covered by a black waistcoat with a high necked collar. Again he was without a cravat, and the lapels of his shirt fell open to expose smooth, tanned skin.

"I'm sorry," Julia stammered. "I didn't mean to pry. I was just bored of being cooped up."

"It's fine." Pushing off the door he strode to her, stopping so close she could feel the heat of him against her bare arms. "You are welcome to make yourself at home while you are here."

"Thank you, your Grace."

"Sebastian."

"What?" She looked up, surprised.

"Call me Sebastian. Since I am forced to use your given name, it's hardly fair you can't use mine."

"Yes, your Grace ... Sebastian." The name certainly suited him, regal and masculine, powerful and seductive—but she felt uncomfortable using it. He was a duke, after all, and she the lowly daughter of a penniless viscount.

"It's good to see you up and about," he ventured, his eyes performing a quick sweep of her figure, no doubt taking in the scandalous fit of her gown. Suddenly she wished she hadn't left the shawl at the other end of the room.

"I ... Mrs. Holland said I was welcome to the dresses in my room," she explained stupidly.

"Indeed. They belong to my sister, Catherine, but she prefers to stay in London these days. Judging from the bills I receive from the dressmaker there, I doubt she is in need of them."

Unsure of what to say, she simply nodded and turned her attention back to the book in her hands. She turned the page gingerly, careful of the worn binding, and attempted to breathe in that scent she had loved since she was a child. Leather and age, it had always put her at ease. At the moment, however, the smell of old books was overpowered by another, more potent scent. Cedar and pine, spice and brandy—it was entirely male. Goodness, he was too close, she couldn't concentrate ...

The book slipped from her hands without warning and she gasped, bending to catch it before it hit the floor. Rutland moved almost before she could react, bending down beneath her to save the precious volume. When he drew himself back up to his full height, he was closer still, the fabric of her gown brushing against his jacket each time her breasts rose and fell with her now-quickened breath.

His face had grown serious, his gaze focused on her with an intensity that made her shiver.

"Julia?" he asked, so close she could feel the warm puff of his breath fan across her cheek.

"Yes?" She tilted her head upward, lashes lowered. Was he going to kiss her? Oh, heaven help her, she wanted him to.

"Let me help you."

"Hmm?" Why was he still talking when he was supposed to be kissing her?

"Tell me what you're so afraid of."

What an odd thing to … oh! Her eyes snapped open and she scowled. He was watching her carefully, his green eyes tinged with amusement; he knew exactly what she'd thought he was about.

With a cough she stepped backward and shook her head. "At the moment the only thing that worries me is you standing so improperly close, my lord." She'd kept her voice even and measured, unaffected. Good.

"My brother is due to arrive this afternoon from London. If you feel up to it, I'd like you to join us for dinner," Rutland said, changing the subject yet again in that disarming way he had.

"Thank you, yes, I'd like that," Julia replied after a pause. Either he hadn't noticed that she'd nearly swooned being so close to him, or he was going to be a gentleman about it and pretend he hadn't.

"You should rest a bit before then, my lady," he commented casually, a slow smile spreading across his features as he stepped back from her. "You look about to faint."

She returned his smile with what she hoped was a murderous scowl. The arrogant rogue! Turning on her heel she lifted her dress and hurried from the room to the sound of his low chuckle, back up the steps and into the safety of her bedchamber. Pulling off her gown, she threw it to the floor with as much strength as she could muster and flopped face forward onto the bed. If only she had a shovel, she'd dig herself a hole in the ground and never come out.

Chapter Three

*W*hat the bloody hell was wrong with him?

His scar flared to life with a throb. Sebastian shook his head and sighed as he replaced *The Iliad* on the bookshelf and strode from the library. Jamming a hand through his unruly hair he cursed aloud, drawing a gasp from one of the maids as she passed by on the way to the kitchen. She scurried off, throwing a worried glance over her shoulder as she disappeared down the hall.

On a normal day he would have been angry with himself for it—he didn't like to show anything but control and restraint. But he was already battling a myriad of emotions, and all over that ridiculous, foolish little hoyden—the one who was decidedly not supposed to be a part of his very ordered life.

She'd expected him to kiss her, and true to fashion, he'd done what he did best: push her away.

He'd done it because he couldn't think of any other way to handle the situation. The only alternative had been to kiss her. He was shaken because not only had he wanted to kiss her, but because he now felt the nagging tendrils of guilt at having been so harsh.

Was she innocent or wasn't she? One minute she was gazing up at him expectantly and the next spouting the standard proprietary drivel that every young debutante possessed in their vocabulary. Christ, she was torturing him.

Or was he torturing himself?

Either way the end result was the same. With that thought

he fought the urge to adjust his breeches. His physical reaction to her was perhaps the most disturbing part; as soon as he'd seen her in the library, barefoot in a gown that was at least two sizes too small for her on top, strands of hair falling from her chignon to brush her creamy shoulders, he'd responded in an entirely male fashion. It wasn't like him to be so ... interested.

Not anymore.

He was saved from any further reflection by a high-pitched, feminine giggle coming from his study, followed by a man's chuckle. His scowl deepened. Alex had arrived.

How very typical of his rakehell brother to seek out female company first thing. But who, precisely, was he sending into such fits? Elizabeth was a pretty girl, and it had never been beneath Alex to dawdle with the servants before. If it wasn't her, though, it had to be ...

"Bloody hell!"

"Sebastian Andrew Cade!" Mrs. Holland materialized from the kitchen, a look of matronly fury on her face. "You mind your tongue with a lady in this house! Duke or not I will tan your hide if I hear that one more—"

"Not now, Mrs. Holland!" he barked and stalked off toward his study.

He threw the door open with flourish, enjoying the resounding 'crack' as it struck the wall and bounced off.

Alex was in the corner of the room, leaning against the wall, his body bent over a small, female form. He turned and lifted an eyebrow with casual indifference. A tiny, round face peeked out from around the coattails of his brother's jacket. The maid gasped and straightened, face flushing crimson. Sebastian couldn't prevent an audible sigh of relief.

"Brother!" Alex grinned and threw his arms open. "Elizabeth here was kind enough to offer me some tea. I was merely introducing myself."

"I'm sure you were," Sebastian bit out.

"Can—can I get ye anythin', milord?" she stammered.

"No, thank you, Elizabeth. You may go help with dinner."

"Yes, milord." The girl curtsied and fled out the door.

"Well, that was poor timing," Alex said once she'd gone. "You sure you need her here, Sebastian? Because I wouldn't mind taking her back to London with me. Quite the treasure, that one."

"What would Lady Abigail have to say, I wonder?" Sebastian moved to the side cabinet and poured two glasses of brandy, handing one to his brother before taking the other for himself and dropping into his chair.

"Ah, Abby and I have parted ways, unfortunately."

"Unfortunate for whom?"

"Why, for her of course." Alex took a sip of brandy and settled into a chair by the fire.

"You go through mistresses faster than Catherine does dresses," Sebastian commented. It wasn't meant to scold, he was far too used to his brother's antics by now.

"I kept her for nearly four months. Far longer than I should have, I suppose. It stopped being exciting after two."

"You mean after her husband found out and gave you his blessing?"

"Exactly." Alex shrugged, downing the rest of his drink. "No fun in having permission."

Sebastian was accustomed to his brother's arrogance by now. It had never shocked him, only reminded him far too much—of himself. Once upon a time he'd had an endless string of mistresses as well. Happier times? Not particularly. But less painful times, to be certain.

"So, care filling me in on why I had to depart London with such haste and come to Foxwaith?" Alex broke the silence. "Your note was quite cryptic."

"I need your help with a … a visitor."

"Female visitor?" The younger man sat up in his chair, suddenly interested.

"Yes, as a matter of fact."

"Who?"

"That," Sebastian sighed, "is precisely what I need your

help with. I've no idea."

"Indeed? A mystery, then!"

"I found her five nights ago, unconscious in my garden."

"Amnesia?"

He shook his head. "No, she knows exactly who she is, she just won't tell me anything beyond her first name. Julia. It seems she was recently in London, though."

"What makes you think so?"

"She blanches whenever anyone mentions it."

"So do you, and you haven't been there in five years." Alex snorted.

"I do not blanch, Alexander."

"If you say so. Alright, Julia from London. Is she attractive?"

Sebastian tried to sound nonchalant. *She's bloody gorgeous,* he thought. "I'm certain someone is missing her."

"And what would you like me to do about it?"

"She'll be dining with us tonight. Don't scare her, but try to see if you recognize her. If you do, let me know."

His brother leaned back in his chair again, extending his legs, one ankle crossed over the other. "Perhaps I can charm her into sharing a bit more about her identity, too."

"Yes." Sebastian stood and turned toward the fire to hide his scowl. He felt the pricks of jealousy in the back of his mind at the image of Julia laughing and giggling at Alex's silver-tongued praise. "Perhaps you can."

Alex also stood, placing his glass on the mantle. "I believe I'll bathe before dinner."

"I'd advise it. You stink of horseflesh."

"Where did you send Miss Elizabeth off to, dear brother? I wonder if she will be so kind as to aid me."

"So you plan to seduce the maid now, and Lady Julia later tonight?"

His brother moved to the door. "Why else would there be so many hours in the day?" Then he was gone, whistling as he moved in the direction of the kitchen.

Sebastian followed a moment later. He'd take a walk around the gardens before returning to his chambers to prepare for dinner. The fresh air would do him good, maybe even clear his head a bit. Lord knew he was in need of it.

Mrs. Holland was waiting for him by the veranda door. He nodded to her, then stopped and waited for the scolding he knew he was about to receive.

"Might I make a suggestion?"

"By all means, Mrs. Holland." He recalled his earlier behavior. He'd have to make that up to her.

"Get the girl some dresses of her own. With your permission, Elizabeth or I could accompany her one day to Grantham. She's not voiced a word of complaint about being in your sister's old things, but I don't believe she is comfortable in them."

"Out of the question. I have no idea who she is, she could be a murderer or a thief or …"

"Your Grace," she cut him off, "you know good and well she's none of those things. She's a charming young woman who is scared out of her wits of something. Perhaps if you showed her some compassion, she would tell you what."

"I've let her stay in my home, that's compassion enough."

"I hardly think it is." She sighed. "I have no right to tell you how to live your life, my lord, but I have known you my entire life and think of you almost as a son, even though I am your servant."

"And you are like a mother to me." Sebastian gave her an affectionate smile. "You know this."

"Whatever happened between you two earlier had you cursing up a storm in the foyer and her sobbing on her bed upstairs. If you want her to trust you, perhaps you must also trust her."

He swallowed hard and looked away. The guilt he'd felt earlier returned tenfold. She'd been crying? Damn. That really had not been his intention. But he had wanted to make her leave him alone, and hadn't really cared, at the time, how he achieved the desired result. If he were to be honest with himself, he hadn't given much thought to her feelings at all, only to his own.

"I can tell you think she's just some silly girl, my lord, and so can she."

Actually, that wasn't what he thought of her, but he stayed silent. It had been years since Mrs. Holland had given him a motherly lecture, and he was certainly due for one.

"She happens to think you are surly, boorish, and uncompromising. I can't disagree with her."

Again Sebastian was silent. He couldn't disagree, either. For the first time in years, that truth bothered him.

•

As if Julia wasn't embarrassed enough at having been driven to tears by Sebastian's harsh comments, being discovered that way by Mrs. Holland had been utterly mortifying. The housekeeper had offered her a comforting hug but, thankfully, hadn't said a word on the subject. A bath was brought up for her, and the warm, rose-scented water helped chase away some of her distress, but it was impossible to completely relax when she knew that in an hour or so she would be face to face with the Duke once again. She wasn't looking forward to an evening in his company, not when his moods changed with such startling frequency.

Only that wasn't entirely true. Part of her did want to see him again. Even if he was horrid to her. And history indicated that he would be.

Well, she resolved as she slipped her head under the water to wash her hair, he could be as cruel to her as he liked, she wouldn't give him the satisfaction of letting it upset her ever again. In fact, she wasn't going to waste another moment thinking of him.

Finishing her bath, she toweled dry and allowed Elizabeth to help her dress in a deep blue evening gown with short sleeves and a scooped neckline. Around the empire waist the maid tied an ivory ribbon, the same color as the gloves she provided. Once again, the dress was too small on top and so they tried with limited success to conceal her breasts with an ivory wrap around her shoulders. Julia's black hair was piled atop her head in tiny ringlets, a few tendrils left down to frame her face and shoulders. She forced her feet into a pair of blue brocade slippers that were also too small and not the least bit comfortable, but she was not about to appear for dinner barefoot.

With a deep breath and one final, nervous check in the mirror, she was ushered out of the bedchamber and down to one of the rooms she had briefly explored earlier in the day. Muted voices drifted to her through the closed door, one lighthearted and teasing, the other lower and tinged with far less amusement. No mystery as to which was which, she thought wryly before rapping her knuckles lightly against the door and pushing it open.

Both men stood as she entered the drawing room.

Alexander was just as handsome a she'd remembered, but she'd also been right about her comparison of the Cade men; he was not as attractive as his older brother. Their features left no question that they were siblings. Alex shared the same striking green eyes and dark blond hair as the Duke, the same square jaw and slightly dimpled chin. His nose was straight and flawless, and no scar marred his cheek, which somehow made him almost too delicate in appearance, too perfect. Julia noted a small webbing of laugh lines around his mouth, indicating that his disposition was decidedly happier than his brother's. His hair was just longer than Sebastian's; she found it ironic that the brother who spent most of his time in society had the unfashionable hair cut, while the one who existed as a recluse seemed more in tune with current style trends.

He wore tan breeches and a matching waistcoat. Understated, but well put together, his attired showed he didn't care overmuch for fashion, but knew he was handsome, and how to dress to his advantage.

For the first time, Sebastian was completely dressed, with black breeches and Hessians, a snowy white cravat tied in a perfect knot at his throat. The collar of his white waistcoat stood tall, just brushing the bottoms of his sideburns, and his overcoat, black to match his breeches and boots, was fully buttoned. Her resolution to avoid thinking about him flew out the window the moment he pinned her with an intense, incomprehensible gaze. There was something, just beneath the surface, that seemed to her almost like desire. She curtsied, dipping her head in acknowledgement and when she again raised her eyes to his face, the heat in his expression was gone, replaced by his usual unaffected veneer.

"You must be the mysterious Lady Julia I have been listening to my brother praise all afternoon." The younger man commenting, moving forward to greet her.

Julia's eyes flicked to Sebastian, who had neither moved, nor changed his expression. "He has been praising me?" she asked, somewhat shocked. Not that she cared if he had been, of course.

"No," Sebastian interjected sharply. "I have not. As usual, my brother exaggerates."

Cad! Ill-mannered, foul-tempered beast.

Alex picked up on her anger and deftly stepped in front of her, blocking his brother from her vision for a moment. Unfortunately, it wasn't long enough to quash her interest.

"Ah, my lady." He flashed a set of perfect white teeth before bowing, pressing his lips to the back of her hand with calculated flourish. It was not proper for a man to actually make contact with the woman's hand, he was expected to merely kiss the air above it, and she shivered at the thrill of his scandalous touch, as well as the way the Duke frowned when he noticed it. "No wonder Sebastian has been keeping you all to himself here. It certainly must be a crime, not to share such beauty with the rest of us."

"His Grace is hardly keeping me, Lord Cade. I suffered an accident on the road and was fortunate enough that he discovered me and offered me shelter until I am recovered."

"I beg to differ; it is we that are fortunate to have such lovely dinner company."

She blushed. Sebastian, she noticed out of the corner of her eye, scowled. He was even more ornery than usual, if such a thing were possible. She scowled back, and was rewarded with a flinch from him when he caught sight of her face.

"Shall we dine?" Alex intervened, pretending not to notice the exchange, though surely he'd seen it. "I'm famished, severely malnourished from all the tarts I'm offered in London. You, my dear, look refreshingly appetizing."

Aunt Margaret had thought him scandalously charming before. If the old woman could hear him now she'd catch the vapors. Julia should have taken him to task for it, but the look of increasing fury on Sebastian's face was just too satisfying. When Alex offered her his arm, she took it, slipping her gloved hand through his elbow with a smile and a tiny nod.

The formal dining room was cavernous and unfriendly, a rectangular, cherry table spanning the length of the room, with a large stone fireplace dominating the far end. A series of portraits lined the walls—the Dukes of Rutland on the left, their Duchesses on the right. Above the mantle rested a painting of Sebastian, standing in the foyer of Foxwaith Manor, one elbow resting upon the balustrade, the other perched casually on his hip. His face looked severe and stern, his eyes sad. Had there ever been a time, Julia wondered, when the man had been happy?

She allowed Alex to guide her into a chair on the left side of the table, then he sat across from her as Sebastian took his place at the head. Julia had the opportunity to study the brothers at dinner. They were as opposite in disposition as they were similar in appearance. Alex was playful, teasing, and flirtatious, while Sebastian barely spoke, just sat brooding, watching the casual wordplay between his two guests.

"Have you been to Almack's at all this season, Lady Julia?" Alex asked over the rim of his wine glass with a smile.

"No, my—" she stopped herself. My aunt Margaret disapproves of the place and will not allow me attendance, she'd nearly said. Besides, her father would never have allowed the expense of vouchers. Whether he was deliberately prodding her for information or making idle chat, she had to be careful lest she give away more clues to her identity. "No. I have not."

"Pity," he replied. "Would you like to?"

"I—what?"

He chuckled. "I would be more than happy to accompany you to a function. Once you are recovered, of course."

Julia thought she heard Sebastian growl. He muttered something under his breath which she could barely decipher, but thought had sounded like …

"I appreciate the offer, my lord," she replied. "But I do not plan on traveling to London. I will be going to Scotland instead."

This time there was no mistaking the comment from the head of the table. "Like hell."

"Come now, my brother, if the lady wishes to go to Scotland instead of London, you should allow me to take her there."

"No." The word was said with the full force of authority and assertion, coupled with a very ducal stare at each of them in turn.

"Am I your prisoner, my lord?" Julia asked, trying not to squirm under his gaze. The tip of her tongue darted out to lick her lips, and she caught the sudden flash of heat in his eyes.

"No, my lady," he replied.

"But wouldn't that be interesting?" came Alex's amused chuckle from across the table.

She neither acknowledged it, nor caught the hidden meaning in his words.

•

"I haven't the slightest idea who she is."

"You just told me you recognized her," Sebastian ran a hand through his hair with an annoyed sigh. They had retired to his study after dinner, Julia citing fatigue and hurrying off to her room. Part of him had hoped she would stay for a while and pass the time. The rest of him was relieved she had disappeared. Dinner had been awkward, to say the least.

"I do. But Christ, brother, have you any idea how many young debutantes are paraded before me on a daily basis? Ever since you started that ridiculous rumor and allowed the ton to believe I stand to inherit your title in a few years time, the sharks have been circling." Alex scowled.

"Well, it may take a bit longer than a few years, but you will inherit the title some day, and you know this."

"Bully for me," his younger brother muttered, downing the remainder of his brandy. "You know, as a second son it's supposed to be me who has the pleasure of choosing not to marry. You, as a Duke, are the one with the responsibilities."

"It certainly hasn't stopped you from running through your allowances at the gaming hells and whorehouses." It was Sebastian's turn to scowl as he recalled last month's accounting. "You could at least hold off until I am dead and it's your own money you're wasting."

"If it were mine, it wouldn't be half as fun."

"Yes, you seemed to be having a great deal of fun with your dinner conversation this evening. I'm amazed she didn't throttle you." I nearly did.

Alex merely shrugged, nonplussed. "Fantastic plan, by the way, putting the girl in Catherine's old dresses."

"How so?" Sebastian's eyes narrowed.

"Well, they don't quite fit in certain areas, now do they?" Alex grinned wolfishly. "Those breasts of hers are to die for."

"I've a seamstress coming in from London next week," he lied, resisting the urge to punch his younger brother for the tenth time that evening. Dear god, that hadn't been the reason he'd refused to get her new clothes, had it?

"You should reconsider."

"Are you certain you can't recall who she is?" He changed the subject.

"Quite."

"Do you think she's someone's mistress?"

"Have you really been out of the game that long, Sebastian?" Alex smiled wryly. "That girl's a virgin if ever there was one."

He let out a deep breath, one he hadn't realized he'd been holding. "You're sure?"

"Well, there's only one way to truly be certain. Would you like me to find out?"

Sebastian clenched his fists at his sides. "I thought you avoided virgins."

"I do, normally. But that one's reputation is ruined anyway, whether she returns to London pure as snow or otherwise. And she is a tempting little thing, don't you agree? I've a feeling that with some proper instruction—"

"You stay away from her, Alex. Don't even think about touching her."

His brother's eyebrows shot up in surprise and sudden triumph. "Hell, Sebastian, if you wanted her for yourself all you had to do was say so."

"I do not want her."

"That's a shame, then, because she's quite obviously taken with you. I'm rather loathe to admit it, but I don't think she'd succumb to my advances anyway—not when she's so desperately waiting for yours."

"She seemed susceptible," he growled.

"Not so," Alex replied. "She only allowed it to continue because she saw it bothered you. Which, I might add, is precisely why I was doing it in the first place."

"The only thing that bothered me was watching you act like such a bloody reprobate."

"Oh, come off it, Sebastian! Just take her to your bed and be done with it already."

"I'll do no such thing!" Sebastian shouted, his anger coming unchecked. The longer this conversation continued, the more he wanted to end it, violently.

Alex laughed. "You won't be able to get her out of your head until you do, big brother. Trust me, I know."

"You still haven't learned to keep your mouth shut, have

you?"

"Actually, it's all I've done for the last five years. I've sat back and watched you wallow in your own guilt for far too long. You weren't willing to find your own happiness, but here it is anyway, dropped right into your lap." Alex moved to the door with a sigh. He wrenched it open, then paused. "When are you finally going to forgive, Sebastian? The only person who ever blamed you for Amelia's death was you."

When the door slammed shut, Sebastian stared at it for a moment, then hurled his brandy tumbler at the space where his brother's head had just been. The glass shattered with a satisfying crunch, shards falling to the carpet and reflecting the light like diamonds. Dinner had been frustrating, not to mention unsettling, and his fury had steadily rose all evening. Striding to the side table, he picked up another glass, then thought better of it and set it down again, picking up the entire bottle and settling into the leather armchair by the fire, taking a long pull straight from the bottle before lighting up a cheroot. He hadn't gotten drunk in years, not since the unfortunate incident with the tavern maid, but if ever there was a night to indulge, it was tonight.

Alex and he both knew of loss, and torment, but the younger Cade hid his pain far better than the older. It had been a love match between their parents, one of those rare and elusive unions amidst the ton. Their mother had died from complications of childbirth. Sebastian had been too young to truly understand what happened, but she had bled giving birth to Alex. There had been an infection, and a few short weeks later, she was gone. Their father was a kind man who loved his children, but he never recovered from the loss of his wife, and though he always swore he did not blame his younger son for it, he could never quite hide the pain in his eyes when he looked at Alex. The young boy knew it, too, sensed it and had always harbored a secret guilt over his existence. It was, Sebastian knew, why he behaved with such reckless abandon. Why he had as much of an aversion to marriage and children as Sebastian did.

Five years ago, Sebastian had been much like his brother was now—cocky, arrogant, and insatiably horny. With his father still alive, he was afforded more freedom, and the lectures about responsibility fell on deaf ears.

He kept a steady string of mistresses to slake his lust, but grew bored easily. Not yet with the weight of the world on his shoulders, Sebastian had cared little for anything beyond that night's diversions, and any evening that concluded with finding release in the warmth of a willing female was one well-spent. He had been on a quest to find a new woman to keep him entertained, but had come across Amelia instead. The daughter of a Marquise, she'd been called the star of the season that year, and when he finally laid eyes upon her one evening at Almack's, he knew why.

He had pursued her relentlessly, charming her at every opportunity. He'd wanted—no, needed—to possess her, and when she had agreed to first his courtship and then his proposal, he'd had no regrets about walking away from bachelorhood. They would marry, and live happily, a relationship based on love and not money or titles. The whole of the ton would envy his good fortune. Most of them already did. Sebastian had told Amelia that he would forgive her anything, would die for her. But it had been a lie. She had done the one thing he couldn't excuse, and he sent her away.

He remembered the desperate look in her eyes, the pleading in her voice as she'd begged him to reconsider. He had cursed her, called her a liar and a whore. The following morning he had received two letters: one from his father summoning him to Foxwaith, and the other from Amelia's father informing him of her suicide.

Remaining in the country had, at first, been necessary to see to his father's funeral and take over the ducal estate. He'd used his new duties as a distraction, pretending that they were the reason he'd locked himself away, and not a broken heart.

Eyes closed, Sebastian tried to call up Amelia's face in his mind. But instead of his dead fianceé's blonde, delicate beauty he saw raven hair, blue eyes, and a heart-shaped mouth.

Damn her. Why had she come? She made him feel again. In her presence, he could almost forgive himself. He could almost forget.

With a sigh, he downed the remainder of the brandy, letting the heat of it burn a path down his throat and cloud his weary mind. She remained, the only thing clear. He wanted her. Perhaps sleep would distract him. Tomorrow he would speak with Alex about taking the girl back to London. If she still required protection from whoever had her so frightened, he could charge his brother with the task.

Sebastian's feet moved of their own accord, past the door to his bedchamber and down the long hall until he stood before Julia's room. What was he doing? He willed himself to turn around and walk the other way. This was trouble. That woman was trouble. Go back to your room and get into your bed, you bloody idiot. But he knew, even before his hand raised and prepared to knock, that he'd already lost the battle. He'd lost a week ago, the moment she had looked at him with those crystal blue eyes.

Chapter Four

Julia started at the rap on her door. What time was it? The fire had died down to nothing but an eerie glow in the hearth. She had been far too distracted to sleep, playing over the night's events in her mind. Lord Cade had made her blush again and again with his silver-tongued flirtations. But each time she closed her eyes Sebastian's stern visage appeared, eyes burning with heat. She imagined him speaking to her as Alex had, whispering scandalous things in her ear.

She wanted that.

The knock came again, louder this time. Throwing off the covers, she shuffled to the door and pulled it open, blinking as her eyes adjusted to the darkness. Sebastian stood in the doorway, filling her vision, hands raised above his head to brace on either side of the frame. His jacket, waistcoat, and cravat were gone, shirt unbuttoned and free of his breeches. His hair was mussed giving him a thoroughly disheveled look.

"Your Grace?"

"Lady Julia." He took the acknowledgement as an invitation, and stepped into the room, brushing past her. Her bare arm tingled where his body made contact. "Are you well?"

The question took her by surprise. "I ... yes, my lord. Thank you."

"After dinner, you said you felt poorly," he explained. His gaze made a quick sweep of her figure, and she was suddenly aware that she stood before him in only her thin, white shift.

"So you came to check on me?"

"No."

"Your Grace," Julia sputtered, making a vain attempt to shield herself from his view. The nightgown she was wearing hadn't seemed scandalous when she'd selected it earlier in the evening, but now, with him just a few yards away, felt downright wanton. "This is most improper."

"As is you being here at all," he replied with a snort. "Do you realize I've already seen you mostly naked anyhow? When I found you, you were less covered."

She gasped. No, of course she hadn't realized! And how dare he mention it. She caught scent of liquor on his breath, noticed the slight slur to his words. The man was in his cups! "You are foxed!"

"That's for sure," Sebastian confirmed with a lopsided grin. "I had hoped that drinking myself into a bloody stupor would distract me from wanting to do this, but it only made it worse."

She took a step back. He countered with two forwards. There was a predatory glint in his eyes, and the same tempting hunger she'd noticed at dinner. "Do what?"

"This." His arms snaked out with startling quickness, not to mention accuracy, wrapping around her waist and pulling her tight against his sturdy frame. She made to protest and he lowered his head, covering her lips with his. Beneath the smell of brandy she picked up on his own unique scent—pine and cedar. A moan tore from her throat, unbidden.

Oh, damn him for doing this to her now. Why hadn't he kissed her earlier, when she'd expected it, wanted it? Why now, when she'd finally begun to reconcile his indifference with her fascination? It had to be the drink and nothing more.

Hot and hard against her, his tongue teased at the seam of her lips, licking the corners of her mouth. She opened for him and he slipped inside, probing tenderly. His hands stroked down her back and settled around her hips before pulling her closer. Julia went willingly, pressing her body against his as her hands reached up to thread through his hair. Were all kisses like this, she wondered, or only the ones with Sebastian?

He pulled away long enough to tilt her head back and trail his lips along the column of her throat, sending delicious shockwaves of pleasure skittering along her skin.

"Your Grace," she whispered.

"Sebastian," he corrected, nuzzling her neck. "Call me Sebastian."

"Sebastian, please." It embarrassed her that the words came out as a moan, not at all the command she'd intended.

"Please stop, or please continue?" One hand slipped up her side, coming dangerously close to her breast.

She shivered. "I don't know."

"My choice then." His lips slanted over hers again, capturing her in a kiss that was neither rough nor gentle. It was firm and demanding, and full of promise. She whimpered, fingers curled at the nape of his neck, and he took the gesture as an invitation, fitting the palm of his hand over her right breast, kneading the pliant flesh. Her nipples tightened as they did in the cold, but Julia felt only heated desire wash through her. Gone was the frigid, stern duke who looked down his nose at her.

He lifted his head away, and she kept her eyes closed, her breathing shallow, as he continued to caress her. She felt a tug, and then he inhaled sharply.

"God in heaven," he breathed. "I knew they'd be perfect."

They? Opening her eyes she glanced down and saw that he had pulled down the neckline of her gown and released her breasts. He was staring at them hungrily, index finger tracing the tip of one, then the other, in reverent circles. She gasped and tried to cover herself but he caught her hands in his and held them at her sides.

"I've been fantasizing about these ever since I saw you in my rose garden. Did you know that?" Before she could reply he dipped his head lower and took one straining peak into his mouth. He dropped to his knees, hands going to her hips to draw her closer as he enveloped her in warm, wet heat.

Stop stuck in her throat. Words seemed to have escaped her entirely and so she stabbed her fingers through his hair, but instead of pushing him away she tried to draw him closer. The sensations he created with his mouth and tongue, and the occasional scrape of his teeth were exquisite, suffusing her with longing and, most of all, power. To see the Duke on his knees, head buried against her breasts, fingers splayed across her hips made her feel powerful, in control for the first time in her life. Never mind that it was wrong. Never mind that she was proving herself to be a wanton harlot. He had come to her because he wanted her and—

Only he hadn't. His actions were fueled by intoxication and nothing more. All other times he'd been in her presence he had ridiculed her, insulted her, and regarded her with cold disdain. Ruined, her aunt's voice chanted inside her head, *You'll be ruined. Ruined, and by a man who cares nothing for you.*

It was the last that spurred her to act, finally, pulling her from the haze of desire that covered her like a warm blanket. She pushed him away and retreated backward until she felt the wooden column of the bedpost bite into her back, putting some much needed distance between them. Sebastian stood reluctantly, hooded eyes lingering on the part of her where his lips had just been, before returning to her face. "What's wrong?"

"If you were sober, would you have come here tonight?" she asked frankly.

"No," he admitted with equal candor.

"Then I would like you to leave."

"What the bloody hell did I do?" He ran a hand through his hair, which promptly fell into his eyes. His breeches were wrinkled from kneeling on the floor, his unbuttoned shirt revealing the smooth ridge of his collarbone and the muscular planes of his chest. In the dwindling embers of the fire, he looked like a Greek statue come to life, all lines and shadows. His eyes gleamed, reminding her of an animal in the dark, a wolf or a cat – hungry.

Julia sighed, righting her gown so that she was covered once more. Her breasts tingled, straining for his lips, his hands. She missed the warmth of him, but wasn't about to let her resolve falter. Because if he touched her again, she would most certainly lose her nerve, not to mention all rational thought. "My lord, if you only want me when you are in your cups, then I would rather you not want me at all."

"Julia …" he began, taking a step toward her.

She held up her hand to silence him, focusing her gaze on the floor. She couldn't look at him without wanting him. "Please, don't. Just go." Before I change my mind.

A long moment passed, before she heard him sigh. The door creaked open, then clicked shut once more. When at last she raised her head, she was alone.

•

The following morning, Sebastian sat in his study, pretending to go over accounting and communications from his solicitor. Mostly, though, he passed the time nursing an unpleasant hangover and replaying his encounter with Lady Julia. Much of the evening was a blur after he had started drinking so voraciously, but he retained a perfect picture of her, disheveled and in a state of half undress, her lips swollen from his kisses, breasts firm and proud.

At first, Sebastian had thought the events of the previous night a wonderful, vivid dream when he'd woken in his bed, still wearing his breeches and boots, head pounding. Then he'd raised a hand to rub at his forehead and caught a whiff of ladies' perfume on his fingers—the same delicate rosewater scent that Julia drove him mad with day in and day out. He'd found his discarded shirt on a chair and raised that to his nose to find it, too, smelled of her.

He'd scrubbed at his skin with vigor during his morning ablutions but still he could smell her, taste her, feel the tiny points of her nipples pressed against his open palms, against his tongue. Damn it if his younger brother hadn't been right;

this obsession of his would only continue to worsen now that his secret fantasies about her had been confirmed. She was, without a doubt, a virgin; he didn't think she'd ever been so much as kissed before given her inexpert responses to him. But beneath the innocence had been incredible passion. She had stopped him, true, and thankfully for God only knew what he would have done if she hadn't, but not soon enough. Not before he'd discovered that she also felt the attraction between them.

The worst part was his utter lack of guilt. Truth be told, he wasn't a bit remorseful about what he'd done.

Alex was gone again, back to London to honor an invitation he'd accepted to a ball that night. He had promised to discreetly inquire about a missing young deb, and perhaps employ a Bow Street runner or two to get to the bottom of the mystery of Julia's identity. It occurred to them both that Julia's family might be keeping her disappearance a secret so as to shield her from scandal, if they knew she had run away on her own. Alex promised to send word as soon as he learned anything, and to return in a week or two even if he hadn't.

A timid knock at the door sent a jolt of pain through his skull. "Come in," he rasped, causing another shockwave. He groaned, praying that it was Mrs. Holland with the remedy she'd promised to have cook brew up, identifying his ailment the moment she'd seen him descend the stairs.

Julia stepped into the room and took in his ragged appearance with a frown. She wore a sleeveless cream-colored day gown, embroidered with pearl accents around the empire waist and scooped neckline. Her hair was pinned back away from her face, but otherwise hung loose, past her shoulders. She drew in a deep breath, and her breasts swelled, to where he half expected them to burst free of her dress. Unfortunately, no imagination was required on his part any longer as his memory kicked into overdrive, reminding him exactly what those breasts looked like. He noted that she was making a point of looking at everything in the room—except him. Her eyes darted back and forth, and she clasped her hands in front of her, one thumb rubbing over the other in an absent, nervous gesture. Sebastian remembered how those tiny hands had felt sifting through his hair, and imagined them caressing other, more sensitive parts of his anatomy. His breeches were far too tight suddenly, and he took in a deep breath of his own, thankful that he was sitting down and not apt to embarrass himself by such a typical, male reaction.

"I would like to talk about my journey to Edinburgh," said Julia coolly, "and when I might resume it."

"You may not," he answered.

"Why?"

"It isn't safe."

"Then provide me with an escort."

"No. I have none to spare." That, at least, was true. He kept a small household, with only the minimum number of servants required to maintain the estate.

"I am a grown woman!" she exclaimed with enough force to make him look up sharply.

"I realize that."

"I am not some feather-headed young girl!"

"Alright," he replied cautiously.

"I find you infuriating!"

"Likewise." He returned to his writing, careful to avoid her gaze lest he allow her a glimpse at the turmoil of his thoughts. It bothered him that she was so disgusted by their encounter. Her discomfort was painstakingly obvious.

"I demand an explanation from you!"

An explanation for what? For refusing to let her leave, or for stripping off her clothes the night before? That was a discussion he didn't wish to have, at least not yet. "Fine. If you're so intent upon leaving, by all means. You're not a prisoner here. Your horse is in the stable, and your 'fashionable outfit' is in your room." Sebastian kept his tone even and uninterested, not bothering to look up or stop writing.

There was a pause. "Thank you, your Grace," Julia bit out,

and left without another word.

Only then did he throw down his pen and sigh. He expected it would take her five minutes, if that, to storm back in. When she did, he'd swallow his pride and explain himself. Or at the least, apologize. Probably. He wasn't used to either activity, but then, he wasn't used to dealing with anyone save his staff and family these days.

But she didn't return in five minutes. Or ten. He waited, and still she didn't appear.

After an hour had passed and she still hadn't reappeared, he went in search of her. Starting in the front parlor, he made his way around the house. He checked the library, the back parlor, the dining room—all empty. His damn valet, who seemed to spend more time hiding than actually working, was as usual nowhere to be found. Finally, he went to the kitchen, and found Elizabeth and the cook preparing for the evening meal.

"Where is Lady Julia?"

"Gone, milord."

"Gone?" he blinked.

"Headed toward the stables a while ago, dressed up as a man again," she replied.

She couldn't possibly have thought him serious! He exited the house and practically ran to the stables, noting as he entered the stout building that the large black stallion was not in its stall. Apparently, she had taken him at his word. He spotted one of the stable hands carrying a bucket of feed in through the far end.

"Did the lady take her horse?"

"She did, your Grace," the boy nodded. "Asked which way was north. I told her an' off she went. I didn't think it was safe lettin' her off by herself, but she said ye'd given her permission."

"Bloody hell!" he cursed. "Saddle Prometheus." There wasn't much of a choice, he had to go after her.

Once the horse was saddled, he set off at a hard gallop,

heading out of the estate on the only road that led north. She had a good start on him, and her horse was an impressive animal, but Prometheus was the fastest stallion Sebastian owned, had won at the races time and again back when he'd been more social. He was confident that he could catch up with her before she reached town, and put an end to this foolishness.

She was the most stubborn little deb he'd ever met. Fire one moment, ice the next. Either extreme was a danger to him. Then again, he wasn't known to be accommodating either, and that seemed to be the problem. Well, when he found her, they would have it out. She could yell at him if she liked; he planned to do the same. He still thought she must be daft to have run off on her own, again, after what had happened to her last time.

It didn't take long to find her. Three miles north of the estate, she was sitting under a tree, her horse tethered a few paces away. Her head was in her hands and he could see her shoulder shaking as he drew closer. Hell. He'd expected to make her angry, not make her cry. He recalled Mrs. Holland's admonition from the day before, that he'd now twice been the source of Julia's tears. He was an ass. His father would have had a fit over him being such a bastard to a woman.

Sebastian brought his horse alongside Julia's, dismounted, and tethered the animal, then turned toward the crying woman at his feet. She hadn't looked up at his approach, but he could hear her tiny, shuddering breaths. She was wearing the ridiculous stable boy outfit again, the collar of the plain white shirt fallen open to afford him a generous look at her cleavage.

"Julia."

"Go away," she mumbled.

"I won't. You can't just go riding off to Scotland by yourself."

"I ca—" her voice broke on a sob and her shoulders heaved again. "Can so."

He ran a hand through his hair and sighed. "That stallion is far too large for you. Did you steal it?"

Her head shot up. Tears clung to her cheeks, which were mottled and red, indicating she had been crying for some time. Wiping her nose unceremoniously with the back of one hand, she scowled at him. "It's my f— father's horse. He cares more for the damn beast than he does me, so I figured he'd at least feel some pain at my departure if I took it. Though I shouldn't be surprised you automatically think the worst of me!"

Her speech grew more even as her shudders subsided, replaced by anger. *Good*, he thought, *anger I can deal with.* "That isn't what I meant."

"I don't care what you meant," she spat.

"Alright. Why did you run off?"

"You told me to go."

"I didn't mean it, Julia."

"You kissed me!" she exclaimed.

"I did." He didn't apologize, waiting instead to see what else she would say to gauge her feelings.

"I have never been so insulted."

"Insulted?" he asked, genuinely shocked. Her response to his kisses hadn't been one of protest.

"You spend an entire week avoiding me, treating me horridly, and then you get drunk and kiss me. As if I would ignore your true feelings just because you were foxed," she sniffed. "You told me once I underestimated your intelligence. Now you underestimate mine."

"My true feelings?"

"You can't stand me."

He wasn't able to catch the laugh before it escaped, and she scowled. "Julia, no," he began. With a sigh he settled himself beside her in the dirt, legs bent, arms resting on his knees. "You were right about the rumors surrounding me. I started them myself."

She didn't say anything, merely watched him with red-rimmed eyes.

"I …" he sighed again. "Something happened five years ago, in London. I haven't been back since. The only people I allow at Foxwaith, other than the servants, are Alex and our sister, Catherine. I'm not accustomed to being social."

"I gathered that much."

"You're a beautiful woman, Julia. I took liberties last night that I should not have, but I must confess I'm not sorry for it." She sniffed again, and he reached out one hand to brush her tears away. Her cheek was soft and smooth, and she tilted her head, leaning into his touch.

"I wanted you to kiss me in the library," she whispered.

Sebastian nodded. "I wanted to kiss you."

Julia raised her gaze to meet his, her blue eyes somehow even more beautiful with the sparkle of tears on her lashes. The urge to kiss her was overwhelming, and he didn't fight it, leaning forward to press his lips against her silky skin. He kissed her forehead first, then each closed eyelid, followed by her cheeks, and finally her mouth, a light brush of his lips against hers. Her arms slid up his chest and wound around his neck before he could withdraw, pulling him closer. So he kissed her again, reveling in the way she parted her lips automatically for his tongue, letting him slip inside, tasting, exploring.

She smelled of roses and tasted of cinnamon, spicy and warm and comforting. Grasping her waist, he drew her onto his lap, and fought the urge to groan as she settled on top of his groin, her firm derriere putting pressure on him in a most enjoyable way.

Sebastian was all too aware of her, every part of her—the rounded curve of her hips beneath his splayed fingers, the points of her breasts crushed against his chest, her fingers in his hair, the silky slide of her tongue tangling with his. When his hands drifted lower to cup her rear she moaned into his mouth. He'd had dozens of women before in much the same position as she was now, but none had reacted with such honest abandon. None had lit his blood on fire the way Julia did.

Not even Amelia.

Too soon the kiss ended with her pulling back, her tiny pants fanning across his cheek as she regained control of her breathing.

Cupping her face in his hands he rested his forehead against hers. "Who are you running from, Julia?" he asked softly.

"No one," came the predictable, almost automatic response.

"Liar. If you tell me, I can better protect you."

"It's not your problem, Sebastian," she murmured.

"It bloody well is!" he blurted. "You are my problem, so anything that concerns you concerns me." Damn. Why the blazes had he said that?

"Only because you feel honor-bound by some nonsensical duty to rescue the damsel in distress."

She was giving him a way out. *Don't take it*, his conscience prodded. Tell her how you feel. "Let me help you, Julia," he urged instead, avoiding the issue all together. "Who has you so frightened?"

"The Earl of Suffolk," she said finally, her voice barely a whisper.

Sebastian did his best to keep his face neutral, but she might as well have kicked him between the legs. His arousal deflated instantly. "Why are you running from him?"

"Because," she trembled as she spoke and he tightened his embrace, "he's evil."

"So I've heard," he replied. "But what are you to him?"

"Betrothed."

Again he felt as if he'd been struck. "I wasn't aware he'd decided to settle down."

"It all happened very fast."

This time he couldn't hide his reaction. He jerked back, holding her at arm's length by the shoulders. God help Thomas Howard if he'd harmed her in anyway. Sebastian wouldn't bother calling him out this time, he'd simply kill the bastard with his bare hands. He already owed the Earl one as it was; the scar across his face throbbed in agreement. "Did he compromise you?"

Julia's eyes widened at his sudden vehemence. "N—no. No, nothing like that. I only met him just last week at the theater. He invited Aunt Margaret and me to sit in his box, but barely spoke to us, though I found him watching me more than once. Two days later he called to speak with my father, and the following day I was told he'd not only made an offer, the betrothal papers had been signed."

"Who is your father, sweetheart?"

"Viscount Hereford," she admitted.

He knew Henry Deveraux, The man had been an acquaintance of his father's until the Viscount had fallen out of favor with the ton and society in general for his overindulgence in gambling and brandy. There had been a scandal after his marriage to some Scottish noble's daughter, and his own father, who had wed for love and valued the sanctity of marriage above all else, had shunned the Viscount along with everyone else. Few things had rankled Sebastian's father, but he'd mentioned his former friend a number of times in Sebastian's youth, and never in a kind light. The old Viscount was likely desperate for a way to avoid Newgate by now, and Suffolk had seen an opportunity to procure himself a very lovely bride.

"I wasn't aware Deveraux had a daughter," he mused, mostly to himself.

"He sent my mother and me to live at the country estate shortly after I was born," Julia replied, her lips dropping into a frown. "And when she died, it was just me and the servants until this year. I hadn't even seen him since her funeral when he summoned me to London for my first season. If I had been a son, perhaps I would have been more useful to him growing up, but as a daughter, I had little worth until I reached maturity and he could marry me off.

"He couldn't even afford to keep the country home, really. My grandfather has paid for its running since I was a child, but he refused to send money directly to my father, or help with his gambling debts in any way. After my mother's death, he wanted me to come to Scotland and live with him and my grandmother, but my father wouldn't allow it. I think he refused out of spite alone. That's why I have tried to reach Scotland. Grandfather would never allow me to be wed to the Earl if I did not wish it."

Sebastian nodded. He understood her urgency now, and said as much. Aware that he still held her by the shoulders, he loosened his grip and skimmed his palms down her arms to clasp her hands, giving each a reassuring squeeze. She leaned forward to rest her cheek against his chest. He wanted to kiss her again, but this felt nice as well, he realized.

"Will you allow me to go to Scotland now that you know the entire story?" she asked, her words slightly muffled by his shirt.

"I'd like to try a different approach than you galloping off across the border."

"And that would be?"

"We send a letter to your grandfather explaining your situation," he said. "If he agrees to help I will escort you to him myself."

"You say that like you think he may not agree?"

Sebastian shrugged. He did his best to tamp down his anger and chase away the images of Thomas with Julia, ones that bore a striking resemblance to a scene from five years earlier. "I've no idea, sweetheart."

"If he doesn't?"

"Then you stay here with me, under my protection. Either way, you don't marry Thomas Howard. Not," he added through gritted teeth, "so long as I'm alive."

•

Julia curled against his chest, enjoying the intimacy of the moment. The tears began again, and slipped down her cheeks unbidden. Sebastian was the first person she had been able to really talk to about her situation, and he had not only listened, he'd understood. He released one of her hands and stroked her hair, murmuring soft words against her cheek. She didn't know what they were, but it didn't matter. The man had her tied in knots, unable to tell which way was up and which was down. Every time she managed to convince herself he was an awful beast he changed, fanned that tiny spark inside her to a flame, kept her from shutting herself off completely.

But would this be any better, she couldn't help wondering. Once again she found herself dependent upon a man, as she had been all her life. And thus far none had treated her fairly. It seemed, however, that Sebastian was in a similar predicament. She got the impression, though his explanations had not given it, that whoever had violated his trust five years ago and caused him to withdraw from society had been a woman.

There were other reasons why he would reject the ton, but for him to also disavow his duty as Duke to marry and produce an heir pointed to the conclusion that his heart had been broken.

She wondered who had hurt him so. This led to silly thoughts, ones she attempted to quickly brush aside. Could she change his mind? Did he care for her? Could he, if given time? No, of course not. If not for her forced acquaintance with a tree branch, she would never have known him at all. If there existed a woman who could heal his heart, it wasn't her. Unless it had been fate that they meet, in which case …

"Oh, enough!" she exclaimed, not realizing until his hands stilled and he started to pull away that she'd spoken aloud. "Forgive me, your Grace—"

"Sebastian," he corrected.

"Sebastian. I was entertaining foolish thoughts, and only sought to halt them."

He chuckled. "Let's get you back and out of that foolish outfit. In fact, I propose we burn it."

"It's surprisingly comfortable," she protested. "Elizabeth told me that her mother wears breeches often, so that she may work in the fields."

"Having never worn a dress, I can't draw an accurate comparison. But it's not so much the trousers themselves that I object to, it's the fit. Those damn things would be too large on me, and I'm twice your size at least."

His grace in a dress was an amusing thought, and Julia giggled. With a chuckle of his own he stood, drawing her to her feet in his arms at the same time, an impressive display of strength that sent a chill up her spine. She allowed him to lead her to her tethered horse, one strong hand resting against the small of her back. He lifted her into the saddle and then mounted his own horse, a large chestnut stallion even larger than hers. They set off at a leisurely pace that allowed both conversation and a chance for Julia to observe her surroundings, which, she realized, she had yet to do despite having been at Foxwaith for close to a week.

"Your horse is an impressive animal, Sebastian," Julia ventured.

He smiled and leaned down to deliver an affectionate pat to the horse's neck. "I've had Prometheus since he was a foal," he told her, pride evident in his tone. "His father was a fine racing stallion that I purchased as a young man and brought here to Foxwaith to breed."

"Do you enjoy the races much?"

"I used to." He sighed. "In my twenties I was very much like Alex is now."

"A silver-tongued rakehell?"

"More or less."

"I much prefer you now, I think. Lord Alex is very charming but …"

"But?" prompted Sebastian, casting a glance in her direction.

"It is difficult to determine the sincerity of compliments from a man who so freely offers them."

"Ah. Then I suppose I should refrain from mentioning how beautiful you look right now," he murmured, and she turned her head in time to catch his gaze sweep from her breasts to her face, a half smile playing on his lips.

Again she blushed. His expression made it clear he was

remembering the previous night, and enjoying the recollection quite thoroughly. "I only dislike insincere compliments, Sebastian."

"I assure you, my brother was quite sincere."

"Yes, but I imagine he is sincere with every woman. Including Elizabeth," she added, "if the way she looked at him last eve while bringing in the soup is any indication."

"Yes, probably." Sebastian rolled his eyes, laughing. "Alex is a rake, and most unapologetic about it."

"Isn't that a characteristic of any rake?"

"It is. But some day, I imagine, the right woman will come along and turn his life upside down. Personally, I look forward to that day."

Julia couldn't help but wonder who had been the woman to change Sebastian. It was foolish and irrational to be jealous of that other woman, whoever she was, and before the resentment could fully blossom, he shot her a sizzling, hungry look that chased it away. She pulled her bottom lip between her teeth and worried it.

Sebastian groaned. "You make me want to kiss you when do that, sweetheart."

"I wouldn't mind," she replied.

"You better mean that," he said, "because as soon as you're off that horse I plan to hold you to it."

As soon as they reached the stables, Sebastian swung out of the saddle and thrust the reins at the young man who stood waiting to care for the horses. He reached her in two long strides, reaching up to grasp her waist and lifting her up and off her mount with almost no effort. Julia was able to marvel at his strength for a brief moment before he pulled her against his broad frame, his lips crushing against hers. There was nothing gentle about the kiss, nothing soft. White hot desire rushed through her, erupting in a needy whimper against his mouth; her hands fisted in the material of his shirt as if she feared he'd withdraw, or simply disappear.

Everything around them fell away—the stamp of horse

hooves, the shuffling footsteps of the stable hands, the pungent musk of hay and animal sweat. Strong fingers closed around the base of her neck, angling her head to better plunder her mouth, the assault merciless and intoxicating. Though he'd kissed her twice before, it still startled her when his tongue delved past her lips to duel with hers.

"Let's go inside," he murmured, pulling away, "and get you changed. After that, I'd like it if you would meet me for tea in the front parlor."

Julia placed her hand on his proffered elbow with a nod and allowed him to lead her back into the house. She ascended the stairs while he spoke to Elizabeth briefly and then, with the young maid's help, changed into another of Catherine's old gowns, this one a deep forest green that complimented her dark hair and pale skin. Once dressed, Elizabeth styled her hair in a loose chignon, and accompanied her down to the front parlor where Sebastian stood before the lit hearth, a cheroot in one hand and a glass of brandy in the other.

He smiled as his eyes swept over her with approval. Then he turned to Elizabeth and held out his hand. She stepped forward and handed him the shirt and breeches Julia had been wearing. "Thank you, Elizabeth. Please bring in some tea for Miss Deveraux."

"Yes, your Grace." She curtsied and left the room, the door clicking shut behind her.

"What are you going to do?" Julia asked, stepping toward him.

"I told you earlier, we're going to burn these."

"It's the only outfit I own. I'm not ungrateful for Catherine's old dresses, but they are a trifle small, and a tad uncomfortable."

"I know. I will take you into town tomorrow to see the modiste and get you some dresses of your own."

"That isn't necessary, Sebastian, really."

"It is," he countered, pulling her against his side in a loose embrace. "You need proper clothing, whether you travel to

Scotland, or stay here with me. As you said, Catherine's gowns are too small."

Julia nuzzled her cheek against his shoulder, enjoying the way his presence engaged all of her senses. "My grandfather will reimburse you I'm sure."

He chuckled and grazed his fingertips across her cheek. "Unnecessary, sweetheart. Even with my brother gambling away his weight in coins each month, I'm in no danger of being a pauper by purchasing you a wardrobe."

He'd called her *sweetheart* several times now, but she still felt a tiny thrill each time she heard it. "My father has been in debt my entire life. I never want to be like him, relying upon others' generosity, and I have no money with which to repay you."

"Then you may pay me in kisses," he replied softly.

She flushed. He seemed an entirely different man now than he'd been just a day ago, affectionate and charming, flirtatious without being over the top as his brother was. Taking the pile of fabric from his hand she tossed it into the hearth and tilted her chin, offering her lips.

"Kisses it is, your Grace."

Chapter Five

Sebastian rose early the next morning, and was dressed and waiting in the informal dining room for Julia to appear for breakfast. He held a cup of coffee in one hand and a cheroot in the other, mulling over the recent complications to his life.

After lunch the day before, they'd spent the afternoon together. First, Julia had written a letter to her grandfather explaining her situation and asking for assistance. Sebastian had also written to the Duke, expressing willingness to care for Julia for as long as necessary. Without giving details, he'd spoken of his own distrust for Suffolk, and his disapproval of the betrothal. The older man would likely see that Sebastian's concern was more than that of a neutral third party, but perhaps it would persuade him to allow Julia to remain at Foxwaith.

He'd spent the remainder of the afternoon showing his guest around the estate, even taking her to view the now infamous rose bush into which she'd fallen the first time he'd seen her. She'd flushed an endearing shade of pink and he'd given into the temptation to sweep her into his arms and kiss her breathless. When they finally separated, he took note of Mrs. Holland standing in the kitchen doorway, and though she shook her head at his impropriety, he caught a hint of a smile as she turned away.

He avoided, as best he could, thinking on the irony of Thomas being her fiancé. The Duke of Rutland did not believe in fate, only coincidences and the occasional opportunity. Julia was a woman in need of help, and he would give it. Any honorable man would do the same. His attraction to her had formed the moment he'd seen her, long before he knew of her connection to the Earl, and his willingness to assist her as well as show her affection had nothing to do with his once friend, now enemy. There was no satisfaction in that aspect of it … Or so he told himself. He had opened part of himself to her because she had finally done the same.

Today he would take Julia into town to visit the modiste as promised. It was not, as she seemed to believe, a matter of him protecting his ducal coffers from overspending – his father and grandfather had both been very business-savvy men, as was Sebastian himself, and his holdings would not suffer from buying a beautiful woman a new wardrobe. Rather, he had an unshakable desire to influence her selections in a way that would ultimately benefit him. His father had often accompanied his mother to the seamstress, a practice that he knew was uncommon amongst the ton, but one that had brought them both joy.

But Julia was not his wife, and the icy shell he'd erected to protect his embittered heart dared not even allow consideration of the possibility. He had told himself repeatedly the night before, while laying awake in bed fighting a raging erection and the near-unbearable urge to go knock on her door, that the happiness he felt around her wouldn't last. She would betray him, as Amelia had, or die and leave him alone, as his mother had done to his father. Sometime just after dawn he made the decision that he would allow himself this brief glimpse of happiness, but he would not, could not, fall in love with her. Some things simply weren't meant to be.

He took one last pull from his cheroot and tossed it into the crackling fire just as the door opened and the very object of his inner turmoil stepped into the room. She wore a modest walking gown, the white muslin under-dress complete with full, loose sleeves, partially covered by a lavender crape tunic, trimmed in lace around the bottom and scooped neckline.

As with Catherine's other dresses, the bodice was too small

and her breasts seemed ready to break free of their confinement any moment. White gloves encased her dainty hands, covering her arms to the elbows. Her hair was pulled back beneath a simple white bonnet, a few ringlets peaking out around her ears. She had applied a light covering of make-up, he noticed, the apples of her cheeks a muted safflower, her pouty mouth a similar shade. The bruise along her temple had faded almost entirely away. She was not the typical English Rose with light hair and soft, warm features. But it was that very contrast, the ebony of her hair and the icy depths of her eyes, that lured him. Sebastian licked his lips and grinned at her. Why was it that when she appeared his doubts—and his good sense—scurried away?

"Good morning."

Her smile was dazzling, and his heart sped up several paces at the flash of perfect white teeth behind full, pink lips. "Good morning," she returned.

"Would you like coffee?" he asked, moving to pour a cup at her nod. "I trust you slept well?"

"I did, your Grace, thank you."

He chuckled and cast her a sideways glance as she took a seat. "How many times now, do you think, have I told you to call me Sebastian?"

"Several." She accepted the beverage with both hands, raising it to her lips and blowing at the surface of the liquid to cool it slightly. "I imagine you will need to tell me several more. My Aunt Margaret taught me that a titled gentleman must always be addressed as befits his station, even if that gentleman is one's husband."

Sebastian didn't bother to hide his amusement. "I'd wager that your dear Aunt Margaret is unmarried."

"What does that have to do with it? She's been amongst the ton far longer than I have, and is a stickler for decorum."

"Even the most rigid of gentlemen prefer the use of their given name from time to time," he told her, leaning forward with a conspiratorial glint in his eye, "particularly in the bedroom."

She flushed several shades of crimson, averting her eyes and studying the contents of her coffee with keen interest. He took a sip of his own beverage, pleased at having achieved his goal.

"You sound like your brother," she muttered, casting him a glance from beneath lowered lashes.

"I enjoy watching you blush."

"It's embarrassing."

"It's alluring," he countered, settling back in his chair, satisfied to discover he hadn't lost his touch when it came to flirting with the opposite sex.

"You don't have to come with me today," she switched the subject. "I can't imagine dress shopping will hold any interest for you."

"On the contrary, it holds a great deal of my interest at the moment. I wouldn't miss it."

Ah, there it was again, he noted with satisfaction as her cheeks colored. She lowered her head and attempted to cover her cheeks with her napkin, but he reached out and caught her wrist with his hand, stopping her movements. When she lifted her gaze to him once more, he winked.

This time, she smiled, and he saw a flash of emotion in her eyes, too brief to identify, but it lingered long enough to stir his blood. "Sebastian," she said softly, "I think I like this new you."

His heart tripped. For a moment, he thought to deny any change. "So do I, sweetheart," he answered instead. "So do I."

•

They set out for Grantham just after breakfast, and though neither spoke much during the journey, the silence was not awkward or unpleasant. She was getting used to his quiet demeanor. Sebastian had elected to drive his phaeton, rather than one of the formal covered carriages. He disliked long rides cooped up, he'd told her, and the pale blue, cloudless sky showed the makings of a beautiful day. The duke's valet, who apparently spent more time hiding and avoiding his duties rather than performing them, was only too happy to have a sanctioned day off. Julia was equally pleased to have Sebastian all to herself, away from the prying eyes of the servants.

She sat to his right on the cushioned driver's bench, one gloved hand holding a white parasol, the other lightly gripping Sebastian's upper arm. He'd donned a black top hat for the outing, and coupled with a black cutaway coat over his white waistcoat and shirt, tan breeches, and Hessians, looked the perfect picture of a ton gentleman.

Julia watched the countryside clip by at a brisk pace, but having spent most of her childhood on a country estate, she was used to the lush green hills of England. Mostly, she watched her companion, who from time to time would glance in her direction with an unreadable expression and a slight half-smile, but mostly kept his eyes focused on the road.

Eventually the trees and sloping landscape gave way to small houses and then the beginnings of a town. Grantham was small, but welcoming, with cobbled streets and snug buildings, certainly far cleaner than the clogged streets of London. St. Wulfram's Church loomed in the distance, its tall gray spire keeping watch over the town.

Sebastian maneuvered the carriage down Main Street, stopping in front of a narrow two story shop where cloth swatches and dresses hung on display in the windows. A wooden sign hung from the atop the door, identifying the place as belonging to Madame Chloe, Modiste.

Before descending from the seat, he tossed a guinea to the young boy who ran out to grab the reins with grubby fingers. "There's another waiting if you keep a good eye out," he said, and the urchin nodded vigorously, revealing a nearly toothless grin. As the boy secured the reins to a nearby hitch, Sebastian rounded the carriage and offered Julia his hand, helping her down the slender step to the street.

"Madame Chloe has worked in London and Paris," he informed as he guided her to the door with one hand on the small of her back. "Catherine tells me that half the ton seeks her out each season, if they can afford her."

"Then why has she set up shop this far from Town?"

"Well, she's a bit ..." he trailed off and grinned. "You'll see."

A bell chimed as he opened the door and gestured for her to step inside, following close behind. She found the inside of the shop mirrored the displays in the window, haphazardous and cluttered, bolts of fabric strewn across every possible surface. The room was awash with finery, designed to entice the ton into dropping their coin; an elaborately carved, tri-fold full-length mirror stood against the right wall behind a round dais. Several dressing screens, covered with Oriental designs, spanned the back right corner. Set at random intervals along the walls, and one smack in the middle of the room, were a series of arm chairs, all of expensive upholstery and construction, but mismatched. Yes, it seemed the shop's proprietor certainly was a bit ... *odd*, Julia completed Sebastian's sentence silently.

The seamstress was a petite woman with wild frizzy brown hair and dark eyes. Though the store was empty save for Sebastian and Julia, she buzzed about the space in a frenzy, muttering measurements and colors under her breath.

Sebastian's mouth brushed warm against Julia's ear as he bent down to whisper, "Ignore the eccentricities, and trust me."

"Eccentricities seem to be a way of life here, my lord," she murmured back, suppressing a smile.

She felt his fingertips graze the base of neck. "My name's Sebastian."

"Not in public, it isn't proper." She blushed.

Finally, the modiste appeared to notice them. "Sebastian!" she exclaimed. "What a wonderful surprise. But who have you brought me?"

"This is Miss Julia Deveraux, my ..." he paused, and his fingers flexed against her neck by way of apology, "my ward."

Julia cringed, but gave a slight nod by way of confirmation. It was a better explanation than the truth, and preferable to him saying she was his mistress, which would be the only other reason he'd take a woman not related to him under his wing.

Madame Chloe dismissed the introduction with a wave of her hand. She circled Julia once, twice, then a third time like a predator stalking its prey. "About time, I'd say. This dress is far too small, and it's entirely the wrong color for you, my dear."

"Well, that's because it's—"

"I know whose it is; I made it. Three seasons ago, in fact." Chloe tapped one finger on her charge's shoulder, then the side of her left breast. Julia let out a tiny shriek and jumped backward. "As if it being out of fashion weren't enough, Sebastian, her bosom is bursting out. You should be ashamed of yourself for letting her in public this way, no matter how much it may appeal to your male sensibilities."

"You know why we're here," he replied, unfazed. At Julia's horrified expression, he winked. She was used to being poked, prodded, and scrutinized by dressmakers, but this woman was shameless. Calling a duke by his first name, not to mention fondling her clients, was no doubt just the sort of scandalous behavior that had her working from Grantham as opposed to Bond Street. "You should have seen the outfit she came to me in, Chloe. Stable boy rags with even more of her top half showing. She looked like a bedlamite."

She stifled a gasp, opened her mouth to argue, and fixed him with a murderous glare. Sebastian simply smiled and lifted one eyebrow in challenge. She clamped her jaw shut again. The man was hopeless, and as usual enjoying her discomfort far too much. Whatever she said would only egg him on.

The seamstress harrumphed and produced a measuring tape from her apron. "You may go and do manly things, Sebastian," she said over her shoulder. "We shall be some time yet."

"This is all on my agenda today," he replied, settling into an overstuffed armchair placed against one wall and setting his hat on his knee. "I suddenly find women's fashion very interesting."

"Not fashion the man's interested in," Chloe muttered.

"I heard that."

"Yes, I rather thought you would."

His reply was barely audible, but Julia was fairly certain he mumbled, "Women."

She made sure her whispered response was loud enough for him to hear. "Men!"

"The dress needs to come off, dear."

Engaged in an attempt to stare down the Duke of Rutland, who sat regarding her with a bemused grin, Julia thought at first that she'd misheard. "Pardon?"

Chloe's sigh sounded like that of a frazzled mother, dealing with rowdy toddlers. "I can't properly measure you in a dress that's two sizes too small. Strip down to your shift."

"You have to leave," Julia said to Sebastian, feeling her face flush.

"I've seen you in your shift before," he countered smoothly.

The flush in her cheeks became a burn. She slid behind the dressing screen with a whimper and a final, pleading glance in her tormentor's direction.

He winked.

Oh, but she was going to let him have it on the drive home. It was one thing to tease her mercilessly in private, but to behave this way in public, whether they were in Grantham or London, was …

Julia suppressed a giggle with the back of her hand. Truth be told, it was rather fun. Her Aunt Margaret would be horrified. The ladies she knew back in Town would be scandalized. But what was wrong with having a bit of fun, really? If Madame Chloe was the gossiping type, her accidental guardian would surely have handled the situation with more care.

When she emerged from behind the screen clad in her shift, she caught Sebastian's gaze and winked right back. His responding smile was genuine.

The modiste set to work taking the measurements, twining the cloth tape around various parts of Julia's body and muttering the conclusions, as well as adding personal observations. Her waist was "slender," her hips "slim," and her bosom "healthy." Through the whole of the assessments, her eyes remained focused on Sebastian; the way he reclined just the slightest bit in the chair, arms draped along the rests gave him an air of casual dominance. He was also watching her, but for the first time she wasn't bothered that he knew she studied him.

Still muttering, Madame Chloe disappeared through a small doorway at the back of the shop, concealed by a worn silk curtain which had clearly, at one time, been one of her masterpieces. When she returned, she carried a bolt of deep red satin stacked atop another of cream lace, and a few reams of ivory ribbon. A young girl trailed behind her, arms so laden with fabric that only the top of her head was visible above the rainbow of dark, shiny colors. It was the first indication the woman even employed an assistant.

Julia was surprised at the choice of shades. "Madame Chloe," she said as delicately as possible so as not to offend, "I'm sure you know pastels are in this season. I was thinking something primrose, or perhaps jonquil."

She scoffed and made a face. "Colors should follow complexion, not seasons, dear. Jonquil would be hideous on you; wash out your pale skin and against that dark hair you'd look downright sallow."

Sebastian prevented any further protest. "Yes, you'd look stunning in the red, Julia."

She turned her head in time to catch his gaze drift down along her curves, smoldering and appreciative. The residual memory of his hands and lips on her skin made her blush, and something in his eyes when they next met hers showed he was thinking of much the same thing. "Yes," he said again and his voice seemed to have lowered, "the red."

"Alright," she conceded. "But I must have something other

than red, as well."

"Why? Very well, then, how about the orange one?" he pointed to one of the bolts still held by Chloe's assistant, who looked ready to topple at any moment.

"The coquelicot? That's for trimming, not an entire dress."

"If you say so."

"I thought you were suddenly interested in women's fashion," Julia teased.

He chuckled. "I am."

Chloe shook her head with a patient grin, like a mother dealing with squabbling children. "I have your measurements. Go ahead and redress, Anne will help if you need her to."

"That's it?" Julia asked, slipping behind the screen again.

"That's it. I work best when I'm allowed to work. I know the styles, I know your coloring, I know your size. I have all I need."

"She needs a full wardrobe," she heard Sebastian say. "Send me the total as usual." He dropped his voice to a whisper and continued speaking, too low for her to hear.

"It unsettles me to know you're whispering," Julia called out.

"Why is that, my dear?" he asked.

"I wonder if you are saying awful things about me!"

He chuckled. "Never, my dear."

She emerged, fully clothed once more, to find him waiting by the door, watching the traffic pass up and down the street, one hand resting on his hip, hat gripped loosely in the other. She studied him in profile for a moment, the angles of his face highlighted by the sun's rays passing through the glass panes of the window before him. The light glinted off his blond locks, and for a brief moment he looked surreal, almost … angelic.

Every time she saw Sebastian, she found him more and more handsome. Her heart fluttered in that telltale way that signaled intense feminine interest. She wondered, quite suddenly, if she was falling in love with her temperamental guardian. How foolish of her. She barely knew a thing about him, save that he could make her melt with a single glance.

"I have to thank you both," Chloe commented without looking up, bringing Julia out of her reverie. The seamstress was behind a table on the opposite side of the room, cutting patterns from a bolt of purple fabric spread across the wood surface. "It's been so long since I've seen it in my shop, I was beginning to lose hope."

"What, bickering?"

"No, dear," she laughed. "Happiness, and dare I say— love."

•

The first delivery of dresses from Madame Chloe arrived only three days later, with a note explaining that she'd made this order top priority, because no young woman should be forced to wear clothing that was not hers, and too small to boot. Slippers from the shoemaker and accessories from the milliner, for which they'd shopped after departing the modiste, and for which Sebastian had paid a small fortune to have made as quickly as possible, came that same afternoon.

Julia immediately disappeared into her room with Elizabeth, emerging a short time later in a simple walking dress and claiming relief at feeling comfortable for the first time since she'd arrived at Foxwaith. Sebastian made a mental note to pen Chloe a thank you for not only her swift delivery, but for crafting the gown in such a way that he was still afforded an appreciative look at his houseguest's figure. Her breasts were no longer bursting from her dresses, but neither were they concealed in yards of needless fabric. Julia commented that the neckline was a bit low for her tastes, but it suited him just fine.

Sebastian had to admit—he was proud of himself. It wasn't just the sense of satisfaction which came from realizing he was still able to charm a woman with as much ease as his younger brother, he enjoyed the lighthearted, playful side of Julia that was emerging. It meant that she was beginning to trust him, and that she enjoyed his company as much as he enjoyed hers.

It was still odd to find comfort in companionship after so long spent in solitude. There was still a part of him that wanted to push her away, but with each passing moment in her presence that voice grew smaller. He was coming to realize, quite simply, that he didn't like to be alone after all. And then, of course, there was the irony of the circumstances that brought Julia to him in the first place.

The urge to kiss her was a constant presence, one to which he succumbed on occasion. He went to great lengths to catch her off guard, sweeping her into his arms when she least expected it—once when they passed through the kitchen, in front of Mrs. Holland and most of the staff, in the gardens near the spot he first saw her, by the stables when they went to take a ride around the fields. He looked forward to those stolen moments, and the way she would melt against him with a breathy little sigh.

The urge to do more than just kiss her was also there, and each night he would lay in bed for hours, staring at the darkened ceiling and doing everything in his power to keep his thoughts from turning to the woman down the hall. He ran through the estate's accounting in his head, conjugated verbs in Greek and Latin which he'd not since his days at Eaton, counted the number of wood panels on each wall of his bedchamber (one hundred and fifteen on each wall save the eastern one with the fireplace, which had eighty-five).

Sebastian knew that were he to give into temptation, she would not push him away. Desire was ever present in the way she looked at him, in the longing glances she cast his way over meals, as they walked through the gardens, when they met in passing amidst the halls. Alex had been right; he couldn't get her out of his head.

He'd spent the majority of the morning in his study going through a batch of correspondence that had just been delivered. Most were bills from London; Catherine had apparently gone on a hearty shopping spree on Bond Street, and Alex had purchased a new stallion from Tattersall's, for no other reason than to annoy the dandy who'd had his heart set on the animal, according to the scrawled note attached to the invoice.

Toward the bottom of the pile was a letter bearing the seal of the Duke of Argyll. Breaking the wax with his gilt letter opener, he scanned the message with a frown. For the first time in days his scar nagged at him, and he knew a headache was not far off. If ever there was an appropriate time for brandy, it was now. Only he knew that if he indulged, his raging hormones would take control and the first thing he did would be just what he'd been avoiding all week. He hated conundrums.

"Bloody hell," he muttered, shoving back his chair and grabbing the letter. The sooner he gave Julia the bad news, the better.

She was in the library, curled up on a settee with her feet tucked beneath her, shoes discarded on the carpet below. The book in her hands was different from the one she'd been reading the previous day, yet another of Catherine's gothic novels, *The Mysteries of Udolpho*. He had never understood his sister's fascination with outlandish, romantic storylines, which in his opinion bordered on the ridiculous with their perfect heroes and pristine heroines. Upon learning that his houseguest also enjoyed them, he concluded it must be a characteristic of the fairer sex, much like journal writing or embroidery.

Julia's face lit up when she saw him. "Sebastian, you're early," she commented. At breakfast he had promised to fetch her for afternoon tea, which was at least an hour off yet.

"Julia," he perched on the empty seat beside her.

Seeing his morose expression, she straightened and set her book aside. "What is it?"

"I received a reply from the Duke of Argyll." He held up the letter, then tossed it to the floor.

"My grandfather," she said with a smile.

"No." Sebastian raked a hand through his hair with a sigh. "Your uncle."

"But my uncle isn't the—" Julia gasped as realization

dawned. "No," she whispered on a chocked sob, pressing her fingers against her mouth. Her eyes squeezed shut and he saw the glisten of tears on her lashes. "Oh, no."

"I'm sorry, sweetheart." He took her hand and drew her against his chest. She went willingly, settling against his shoulder.

"When?"

"Three months ago."

"What? Why weren't we notified?"

"It seems your father was told." At that she let out another sob, and he felt her shoulders tremble.

"And my uncle won't help me."

"No." He left it at that. Argyll's missive had been short, harsh, and to the point. He'd never liked his brother-in-law the Viscount, and was of the opinion that if his sister hadn't become pregnant, she would not have stayed in England. Though he sympathized with his niece's lot in life, it was nothing unusual to marry the gentlemen of one's father's choosing. Argyll agreed to remain quiet about where she was, but that was the extent of his willingness to help.

She sniffed. "No wonder my father was suddenly in such a haste to marry me off. My grandfather was never willing to provide financial support to my father, but he did ensure that I kept the country estate for my dowry."

"I'm sorry," Sebastian said again, grazing his knuckles against her cheek, smoothing away her tears. "I told you we'd figure something else out if we had to."

"Like what? He was my only chance."

"He wasn't." Had she forgotten the promise he'd made? He would do everything in his power to see that she never married Suffolk.

"I can't stay in the country hiding forever, Sebastian."

"We will figure it out, sweetheart. You have my word." Drawing back he pressed a kiss to her forehead. "For now, though, I say we take our minds off all this."

Julia drew a ragged breath. "How?"

"Change into your riding habit and meet me in the stables. I want to show you something."

Chapter Six

An hour later Julia made her way to the stables with a heavy heart. Poor Elizabeth had applied rogue to her cheeks three times before abandoning the idea; she couldn't stop crying it off.

Her riding habit was a dark Pomona green with long, full sleeves and swansdown trim along the waist, high neckline, and cuffs. Her kid gloves and sandals were boldly done in black to match the soft beaver hat, which sported a single matching feather. She also now had a corset that fit, and while she was glad to no longer feel so exposed, she almost wished Madame Chloe had saved it for the second shipment; she hadn't missed being unable to breathe. Though the outfit was not of a bright happy color by any means, it was too vivid for the occasion. Julia had no mourning dresses. Then again, she noted bitterly, her grandfather had been dead for three months and all the while she'd been flitting around Town in pastels and feathered hats, laughing and dancing and flirting. And Father had known! Oh, if it was possible for her to loathe the man more than she already had, she did.

She rounded the corner of the stables to find Sebastian waiting with Prometheus, his large grey stallion, and Cathy (named by Alex after their sister, apparently) the bay roan mare that had served as her mount all week. Her father's black stallion stayed in the stables, well cared for by the staff. She paused a moment to take in Sebastian's well-tailored form—it had become a ritual for her to catalog his features on a daily basis, partially because she enjoyed them so, and partially because she feared any moment with him might be her last. He was currently bent over examining Prometheus' right fet lock, the tails of his coat parted awarding her with a generous view of his muscular thighs and rear. Funny, she'd never noticed just how snug men's breeches were before.

"That's a pleasant sight," she quipped boldly, and though she managed to say it without faltering, she felt the heat flush her cheeks.

Straightening, he turned to face her with a lopsided grin. "Why Miss Deveraux, what a scandalous thing for a young lady to say."

"Desperate times, your Grace," she replied.

Closing the short distance between them, he grasped her chin between his fingers and tilted her face upward, planting a light kiss upon her lips. "You've been crying," he commented with a frown.

"My grandfather has been my only ally since my mother died. I miss him."

"I know, and I don't wish to diminish that in any way. But realize that now, you have me as your ally."

"I do." At that moment, it was true. There was nothing but honesty and affection in his clear, green eyes. His scent enveloped her, comforted her, and on impulse she lifted her index finger to trace the scar along his cheek. His skin was warm and smooth, freshly-shaven. "Sebastian," she murmured as her fingertips brushed his bottom lip, "please, kiss me."

He groaned, a raw, masculine sound low in his throat and covered her mouth with his. She parted her lips and allowed him entry, trembled under the gentle assault of his tongue. Yes, she believed he would help her. In his arms, the loss of her grandfather didn't hurt quite so much. When he released her and pulled away, it was she who groaned.

"Any more of that and I'll have to bring Mrs. Holland with us to chaperone," Sebastian said before helping her into the saddle and then mounting his own horse.

The pair set off west across the estate, where a neat line of trees lined the base of a steep ridge. Over the past few days, Sebastian had shown her a good portion of his land, but they had yet to explore this direction. She loved it out here; it reminded her of where she'd spent most of her youth, with her mother and a modest staff not unlike the one here at Foxwaith. She'd often daydreamed about the lavish, fast-paced London life, but after finally experiencing it, she realized she enjoyed the quiet solitude of the country.

Or perhaps it was the company. She brought a gloved hand up to her lips, slightly swollen from Sebastian's kisses. She knew he meant it when he spoke of wanting her, could see it in his eyes. Were he ever to break that unspoken boundary and do more than just kiss her, she wouldn't resist, and she sensed he knew it.

It was good he had the sense to control himself, because she did not. To be desired by a man as handsome and powerful as the Duke of Rutland was intoxicating and addicting. It was a two-way street, of course, and she imagined he had twice the hold over her that she had over him. He didn't love her, she knew. But he at least wanted her, and Julia would take what she could get.

Reaching the crest of the hill, Sebastian slowed Prometheus to a halt, and allowed his guest to take in the view. Off in the distance was another large ridge, and between it and the one they stood atop were swells of hills, groves of trees, and squares of fields for farming. A spider web of roads networked across the landscape, with cottages and farm buildings scattered at random intervals. Smoke curled from the chimney of the closest home, and she could make out several figures below, moving about the yard.

"Are these your tenants?" she asked.

"Only some of them," Sebastian replied. "My father allowed many of the farmers to buy their land from him over time. I continue the tradition. Most of the revenue for my estate is from business holdings—shipping and trading with America.

The family coffers are secure, and there's no need for so much land when others have use for it."

With a click of his teeth he urged Prometheus into a walk, and Julia followed suit, bringing Catherine alongside the large grey stallion. "Are we going to visit someone?"

"I come down once or twice a month to check on everyone. When we were in Grantham the other day I ordered shoes for one of the families who was in desperate need of them on my last visit. I'd like to make sure they arrived."

"You still provide for the people, care for them?"

"Of course." He shrugged. "They're good people, for the most part. They've been loyal to my family and we, in turn, are loyal to them."

Julia mused, "So it's not all people you hide from. Just the ton."

Sebastian made a noise in his throat that was either a snort or a growl. "Exactly. Most times I feel I have more in common with these people than my so-called peers. Born on the same land, what separates me from them, other than accidental circumstances of birth?" Gesturing to the small home closest on their left, he said, "John Bowers lives here with his wife, Ellen, and their three daughters. His grandfather was the first of the tenants to become a yeoman. Each year after the harvest, they bring fresh hay to the manor for the horses, and each Christmas I have Mrs. Holland cook a hearty dinner for them, and deliver it myself. I can speak freely with them, without fear of Ellen orchestrating a match with one of her daughters. I'm free to be ..."

"Yourself."

"Yes. It's a rare luxury."

It shouldn't have hurt to think he wasn't free to be comfortable or genuine with her, but it did. "You can be yourself around me, can't you?"

Sebastian didn't answer for a long moment. "Oddly enough," he said finally, "I think I can."

"And why is that odd?"

"Because you were hardly honest with me when you first arrived at Foxwaith. I didn't even know your name."

She bit her lip and dropped her gaze to her hands. "I didn't know where I was when I woke up. I didn't know you, Sebastian, save those unsavory rumors you started." She picked at an errant thread poking from the seam of her gloved index finger. "For all I knew, you were going to send me right back to Thomas, or let him know I was here. I couldn't let that happen."

"I understand." His hand covered hers and squeezed. "There's no comity between Suffolk and I, rest assured."

She snapped her head up. "So you do know him."

"We were acquainted years ago at Eaton." His tone was evasive. Julia sensed there was more to the story but decided to drop it. Sebastian was a man who liked his secrets, regardless of how they plagued him.

Passing through the crudely constructed wooden gate set within the fence that surrounded the Bowers' home, their awkward silence was interrupted by the approach of a burly man with closely cropped red hair and a full beard. Julia guessed he was in his mid-thirties, not much older than Sebastian, though a lifetime of tending the land had aged him faster than the Duke, and his skin was weathered from constant days in the sun.

"Yer Grace!" he exclaimed with a smile, taking Prometheus' reins in one beefy hand. "Mrs. Bowers weren't expectin' ye 'till next month. Just stew today, but I imagine there'll be enough for ye and the lady."

"There's no need for that, John," Sebastian replied, dismounting his horse before assisting Julia down from hers.

"There certainly is," the man replied, "after puttin' me whole family in new shoes, milord, the least we can do is feed ye."

"Ah, good, so you got them. I assume they fit?"

"Very well, milord. Only problem we 'ave is getting' little Mary to take off those fancy lady slippers. She wears 'em to bed an' all."

Sebastian laughed jovially. "My apologies for the trouble, John."

"Come, milord, you must stay and visit for a while. The lady, too."

"This is Miss Deveraux. She's a guest at Foxwaith."

"Milady," John nodded and gave her a gap-toothed smile. "Any friend o' his Grace is a friend o' mine."

"Thank you, Mr. Bowers." Placing a gloved hand on Sebastian's proffered arm, she allowed herself to be led into the house via the back door, which deposited them into a small, but tidily kept kitchen.

The woman at the hearth was slender and unusually tall, with a mess of frizzy blonde hair about her face and shoulders. She had a small nose, freckled cheeks, dark chocolate eyes, and laugh lines around her eyes and mouth. Julia thought she was very pretty, though not in the sense so prized by the ton.

"Yer Grace!" she exclaimed with a smile and a bow of her head.

"Nellie, this 'ere is Lady Deveraux, a friend o' 'is lordship," John said by way of introduction. "Milady, this is me wife, Ellen."

Ellen curtsied, and her smile widened as she looked in Sebastian's direction. "My lady."

"Mrs. Bowers, it's so nice to meet you."

The older woman scoffed and waved her hand. "None o' that please, milady. It's just Ellen, or Nellie, if you please."

"Only if you call me Julia."

"Oh, I couldn't, ma'am. Isn't proper to speak to a lady o' station in such a familiar way."

"I insist upon it." Sebastian found her hand and gave it a squeeze. She knew he was happy with her, and in truth it was easy. The Bowers seemed so welcoming and friendly, she felt instantly at home.

"Yer Grace, the shoes are wonderful. Thank ye so much." Ellen moved to a small hutch and withdrew a stack of bowls, then a handful of spoons, placing them on a low, wooden table at the corner of the room.

"You're most welcome, Ellen," Sebastian replied. "Though I hear Mary refuses to take off the slippers."

"She did, until this mornin' when I told 'er that while ladies do wear slippers, they don't stink to high heaven. She took 'em off long enough for a bath."

Julia giggled. As if on cue, a young girl of about six came tearing into the kitchen, two older girls hot on her heels. All three were the spitting image of their mother.

"Milord!" the youngest squealed and launched herself at Sebastian, who caught her easily, spun her around in a circle and set her back down once more. Upon seeing Julia, she paused. "Who are ye?"

"Mary!" her mother exclaimed in horror. "Mind your manners."

"This is Lady Julia," Sebastian supplied, tousling the girl's hair affectionately.

"Are ye a real lady? From London?"

"Mary!"

"Yes," Julia answered, smiling. "I'm here visiting."

Ellen pulled out the chair at the head of the table and ushered Sebastian into it. She seated Julia to his right, and began filling the bowls with a hearty beef stew. The spicy aroma wafted upward and Julia's stomach growled. John Bowers took the seat at the foot of the table, and the two eldest girls followed suit. Only Mary and her mother remained standing; the former behind the chair to Julia's right, and the latter fetching clay cups for ale.

"Are ye goin' to marry Lord Sebastian?"

"Mary!" This time it was both her parents and her sisters who scolded.

"I'm visiting," Julia repeated, feeling awkward. She kept her eyes on the girl, but she felt Sebastian's gaze on her.

"Humph. I think ye should marry 'im," Mary replied, flouncing into her chair. "That way ye can come and visit me often, and tell me all about the latest fashions. And maybe, one day, ye could take me to London."

"Well, I can do that regardless," Julia said. At last she dared to glance at Sebastian and found him regarding her with bemusement, eyes sparkling.

"True," Mary tilted her head and thought a moment. "But I still think ye should marry 'im. If nothin' else, ye'd have pretty babies."

"Mary!"

•

Sebastian and Julia left the Bowers home late that afternoon, with full stomachs and light hearts. John Bowers was only a few years older than he was, and they had played together as children despite the class differences between them. Eventually, Sebastian had been sent off to Eton for his education. He returned to find his childhood friend married to the vicar's daughter, and blissfully happy. In truth, Sebastian had always been envious of them. Despite the wealth, title, and prestige, he'd never been so content in his life as they were.

Spending time with his humble neighbors always lifted his spirits, and he was glad to see the family had the same effect on his guest. He didn't want to trivialize her grandfather's death. He knew how devastating it was to lose a loved one, particularly when that person had been a steadfast ally to her, but he hated to see her so distraught. Her tears tortured him. For the moment, at least, she'd put aside her grief.

She had seemed so natural in her interactions with the Bowers girls, particularly little Mary. The child's candid questions had persisted throughout their visit, and Julia's face had remained a continuous shade of crimson. For his part, Sebastian found it nearly impossible to contain himself, and when Mary asked if Julia had ever "kissed a gentleman" he'd lost all semblance of control, laughing until his stomach hurt. His beautiful companion had kicked his shin under the table and calmly informed the table that she had not ever kissed a gentleman, strong emphasis on the word "gentleman." This, of course, only made him laugh harder.

The jovial mood was, unfortunately, short lived. As they drew within sight of the stables, Sebastian saw an elaborate, gilded coach parked alongside the building. The crest affixed to the side was unmistakable. Julia's sharp gasp informed him that she recognized it as well.

He'd known that sooner or later, someone would come for her, and he wasn't surprised that the Earl of Suffolk had made the trip personally, but the timing could not have been worse.

"He's likely waiting for us in the front parlor. We'll enter the house through the kitchen, and you can slip up the back staircase to your room. I'll handle him," Sebastian said, bringing Prometheus to a halt and swinging down from the saddle.

"No," Julia replied as she placed her hands on his shoulders and let him lower her to the ground. "I will come with you and speak to him as well."

"That's not necessary, Julia."

She signed and smoothed the lapels of his coat with her hands. "He obviously knows I'm here. I can't hide."

It was Sebastian's turn to sigh. He didn't want her upset again, but there was another reason he'd prefer she wasn't there, as well. There were things about his past he hadn't shared with Julia. "Very well."

Entering the house via the rear, Sebastian spoke briefly with Mrs. Holland, and told her to make sure Suffolk's carriage was ready and waiting on the front drive. With any luck, his visit would be a short one.

Thomas Howard, Earl of Suffolk and the only person Sebastian had ever truly hated, stood before the lit fireplace of the front parlor, a tumbler of brandy in one hand and a cheroot in the other. Turning at the sound of the door, he took one last drag of tobacco and tossed his smoke into the fire. He was tall, but not as tall as Sebastian, with curly brown hair and a hawkish nose. Women thought him handsome, Sebastian knew, but there was a cruel gleam to him hazel eyes and his mouth was set in a perpetual sneer. "There you are, at last," he said in greeting.

"At last?" Sebastian replied. "We were hardly expecting you, Suffolk."

"You should have been. You've kept my fiancée hostage for more than a week."

Julia stepped forward, hands balled into fists at her sides. "I'm not a hostage. I left London of my own free will, and you are not welcome here."

"Left, did you? Whatever for?"

"You know damn well why I left," she stated, and Sebastian couldn't help but smile. So far, she was holding her own against Suffolk quite well. He was proud of her.

"You may have lost a bit of your wide-eyed innocence, but you've gained some fire, my dove. I find that even more appealing. It's been a while since I've had a challenge." If he was unnerved by Julia's vehemence, he didn't show it. "About five years, actually," he added, his eyes sliding to the duke with a smirk.

Sebastian nearly lost the thin hold on his temper. He'd known it was coming, but the foresight didn't do anything to keep him calm. Julia cast him a sideways glance, and he knew she sensed his restraint was slipping.

"How did you find me?" she spoke up, changing the subject.

"Lord Cade," Suffolk revealed. Dammit it to hell, was Alex really that stupid? "He was overheard by Lord Marbury speaking to Lord Anderson about how you have been entertaining a very enchanting, very mysterious Lady Julia. Lord Marbury tells his wife everything, and she in turn shares the gossip with me, as she shares my bed."

Julia gasped. "But it was Lady Marbury who introduced us."

"Indeed, precious. She did so at my request, though I imagine she only complied because she's anxious for a turn with you herself, and knows that I would permit it, so long as

I am allowed to watch."

At her horrified expression, he laughed. "Rutland, I'm disappointed in you. You've barely schooled the chit at all. You've had her here days and days now, and unless I miss my guess, she's still a virgin."

"Unlike you, Thomas, his Grace is a gentleman."

"Ah. Now that sounds familiar. I believe Amelia said the same thing, once upon a time. Isn't that right, your Grace?"

"You sound jealous, Lord Suffolk. Even without a dukedom, Sebastian would be twice the man you are!"

"Ah, she is a fiery little thing. Isn't she, Sebastian?" His chuckle was low and sinister. "It'll make her very passionate on our wedding night, I imagine."

Sebastian took a step forward, pinning the other man with a murderous glare. Julia's hand on his upper arm was the only thing that stopped his progress.

Suffolk grinned. "I'd forgotten how much I enjoy seeing you jealous, old friend."

"We're not friends," the Duke growled.

"No, I suppose not. But it doesn't matter either way. We're still betrothed. She's mine, whether you like it or not."

"I'll never be yours," she said angrily, her grip on his arm tightening.

He laughed. "You're thoroughly ruined, darling, whether he's touched you or not. You have no choice but to come with me."

"I will stay here with Sebastian for the time being."

"You prefer a shell of a man, hellbent on revenge against me? That is," he paused and slid one finger along the column of her throat, "assuming he's told you about his past."

"His past does not matter."

"Oh, but it does, Julia. And if he has not seen fit to tell you, then it seems I must. I'm sorry to tell you, Sebastian never wanted you for you. He wanted you because you are mine." His hand came to rest on her shoulder. "That poor gel who took her own life five years ago did so not because of me, darling, but because of him."

"No," Julia protested. "No, Aunt Margaret told me this story. You compromised her and ruined her reputation, and that is why she took her own life."

"I took her virginity by consent, that's true. I asked for her hand. I, too, loved her. She declined. When her fiance—that would be your valiant savior here—learned of our tryst, he declared her a harlot and called off their marriage. That is why she killed herself. So you see, once upon a time I took something of his, and now he wishes to repay me by taking something of mine. You."

"You lie," she hissed. Sebastian felt her tremble, and saw the shadow of doubt cross her face.

"Ask him, then. Fortunately I am more forgiving than his Grace, and any scandal your hasty flight may cause won't have me crying off. When you realize the mistake you've made, I'll be waiting." Gathering his hat and gloves from the arm chair by the fire, Suffolk offered a mocking bow before striding from the room. Several moments later the front door opened and shut, and the clap of horse's hooves outside signaled the rumbling departure of the earl's carriage.

Slowly, Sebastian turned to face Julia. He half expected to see her in tears, but her eyes were dry. She stared into the fire with an eerie calm that unnerved him.

"Is it true?" she finally asked on a whisper.

He dropped his gaze to the floor before answering and raked a hand through his hair. It was one thing to avoid the subject, but when confronted so directly, he had no choice but to be honest. "Yes."

•

Her heart broke at that simple admission. She hadn't realized just how far she'd fallen for him until, with one small word, he'd set the entire world crashing down around her. She had hoped he would deny it, would confess his love for her but the moment Thomas had mentioned the other woman, Amelia, Julia had seen Sebastian's face cloud with emotion. And she'd known from the beginning, of course, that he had secrets.

Refusing to look at him, she kept her gaze trained on the fireplace. Watching the orange flame lick at the pile of logs, then twist and dance higher, somehow kept her calm. It kept her from bursting into tears which, she silently vowed, would not happen until she was alone. The Duke of Rutland had broken her heart, but she wasn't about to give him the pleasure of seeing her cry a second time today.

"I knew you were keeping something from me," she said finally, keeping her voice low and composed. "But not even for a moment did I suspect this. To think I ran from one scoundrel straight into the arms of another."

"Julia, it isn't that simple. Let me explain. When I said—"

"I don't care to hear your explanation, Sebastian. I'm not certain I can believe any you have to give." No, she wouldn't allow him to charm his way out of this one, as he had done more than once before. "I believe I'll retire to my room now."

"Please, Julia, allow me to—"

Again she cut him off, moving toward the door with as much grace as she could muster. Any moment now she would fall apart. She had to get away from him, as soon as possible. "I said no. If you'll excuse me, your Grace."

She half expected him to follow her, but he didn't. She heard his muffled curse as she slammed the door behind her and made her way through the foyer. When she reached the stairs, the first splash of tears hit her cheeks, and she began to run.

Once safely within the confines of her bedchamber, she let out a sob. She was a fool. All the things her father had called her—simpering, idealistic, shameful. How idiotic to think a man like Sebastian could ever care for her. He was a man who hid from society, who loathed the ton so acutely that he'd rather the whole world think him a disfigured monster than be forced to socialize with them. Was it even possible for a man so broken to care for anyone? And here she was thinking that he could love her! Sebastian Cade loved nothing, not even himself.

Rummaging through the wardrobe set against the far wall, she withdrew the small valise she'd found her first day in the house and began to fill it with the dresses Madame Chloe's assistant had delivered. Once she reached her destination, which at present was defined as anywhere but Foxwaith Manor, she would return the clothes and luggage. But for now, she needed them. His Grace could consider it payment for her unwitting complicity in his scheme.

The door creaked open, startling her. She shrieked and whirled around, mentally bracing herself for a confrontation with the duke.

"It's only me, dearie." Mrs. Holland shuffled toward the fireplace. "I came to light the fire for you, didn't realize you were in … Oh heavens!" she exclaimed, catching sight of Julia's tear-stained face. "What's he done now?"

"He hates me."

"Oh, now, I doubt that, child."

Julia shook her head and set to folding the gown she pulled from the armoire.

"What's this, now?" Mrs. Holland came to stand beside her, nodding to the open suitcase.

"I'll return everything."

"You can't go running off in the middle of the night," the older woman told her calmly.

"I can't stay here any longer. N-not …" Julia's voice broke.

"I'll tell you what, dear, promise me you'll stay the night. Tomorrow morning, if you still wish to go, I'll see to it you travel safely with William, his Grace's valet." As if to prove she'd accept no protest, Mrs. Holland helped Julia out of her riding habit and corset, leaving her in her shift. She felt some instant relief at being out of the restricting clothes. It was no wonder women succumbed to the vapors in difficult situations, ladies' dresses were not conducive to extreme emotions.

Sebastian had a valet? In the time she'd been at Foxwaith, she'd never seen him. "I d-don't wish to see him."

"I know. You won't have to."

"Promise?"

"I promise, dear. Here, I'll give you the master key to the house. Lord Rutland lost his ages ago." Mrs. Holland produced a small brass key from her apron and set it on the nightstand, then patted Julia's hand and helped her into bed, drawing the covers up to her chin. "Now, have a rest, and in the morning we'll sort everything out."

Chapter Seven

Sebastian approached her room with even steps, determined to repair Julia's tarnished opinion of him. How she could ever believe he was only using her to exact revenge wounded him far deeper than he'd thought possible. That she trusted him so little, was so quick to condemn him, only served as a reminder of all he'd finally hoped to put behind him. He wouldn't allow it to happen again, not when she'd so nearly brought him back to his old self.

When he reached her door he hesitated, hand resting on the knob in a too-tight grip that made the smooth polished brass bite painfully into his palm. What would he say to her?

The truth. That revenge had crossed his mind upon first learning of her circumstances. That he was very likely falling in love. That he'd die before he harmed her.

Taking a steadying breath he twisted the knob and found the door bolted. Locked? Sebastian resisted the urge to punch something. After finally recognizing the depth of his feelings for her and gathering the courage to declare them, she locked him out. How dare she!

He rapped his knuckles on the door.

"Go away," came her muffled reply.

"I can't. Let me in, Julia, so that we might talk about this."

"No."

"Julia, unlock this door," he bellowed, pounding one fist against the wood.

"I will not!" she shouted back.

"Open the door or I'll break it down!"

"Go right ahead! It's your damn door!"

He clenched his jaw. The scar along his cheek throbbed painfully, and for a moment it felt as if the old wound had reopened. Fine. If that was how she wished to act, he'd try a different approach. Storming down the stairs he found his housekeeper in the kitchen, brewing a pot of tea and humming softly.

"Mrs. Holland," he boomed, startling the older woman.

"Your Grace," one gnarled hand flew to her throat in surprise. "What can I get you?"

"Your master key." He'd lost his long ago and hadn't bothered to replace it.

She sighed. "She doesn't wish to see you, milord."

"I'm aware of that."

"Best give her a day or two to calm down."

It was a wise suggestion, but Sebastian was all too aware of Julia's penchant for irrational plans when it came to unpleasant situations. "I doubt," he said wryly, "that I have that long."

"I promised her she would not have to see you tonight."

Well, that was interesting. Was he facing a mutiny amongst his staff? "You shouldn't have," he said with a scowl. "I'm afraid you're about to break that promise. The key, Mrs. Holland."

The woman sighed again and shook her head. "I don't have it, your Grace."

"Where is it?"

"I gave it to the lady not twenty minutes ago at her request."

Perfect. Now he really would have to break the damn door down. Spinning on his heel he stalked up the back stairs, trying to calm his temper. He took a deep breath once at his destination, and brought a hand up to rub at his forehead.

"Miss Deveraux," he announced as sedately as possible, "you have one last chance to open the door."

"Go to hell!" she shrieked.

Under any other circumstance, he would have found her

sudden adoption of profane vocabulary amusing, but since it was directed at him, he missed the humor in it. Curling his fingers into his palms he took a deep breath, stepped back, and rammed his shoulder against the door with the full force of his body weight, which was not unsubstantial.

The impact jarred his skull and he swore. Stepping back again he repeated the process. On the fifth try the door splintered at the hinges and on the sixth pass it gave way, crashing to the parquet floor inside the room. Bloody hell, that had been harder than he'd expected, and he could now add a sore shoulder to his growing list of aches and pains. He wondered if any of the authors of Julia's beloved novels, who constantly wrote about heroes crashing through doors to save the damsel in distress, had ever tried it themselves.

Julia was in bed, hidden beneath a massive pile of blankets that could only have been Mrs. Holland's doing; when he was a boy, she'd often buried him to near suffocation with blankets, calling it good for the soul. The riding habit was slung across the top of the dress screen in the corner of the room, which told Sebastian his beautiful guest was likely clad only in a shift. Damn those blankets! Her hair had not been taken down, and it was in a state of disarray, half pinned, half loose, sausage curls falling around her cheeks, which were mottled from crying.

She stared at him with wide eyes, one hand drawing the covers up to her chin. "My god, you've gone mad. You broke the door down," she whispered, gaze darting from him to the pile of splintered oak around his feet.

He snorted. "I don't make idle threats, Miss Deveraux."

"No, just empty promises."

"Damn it to hell, Julia." He almost added, *You are trying my patience*, but realized, standing on the remnants of her bedroom door, that patience wasn't something he currently possessed.

"Are you going to …" she trailed off, leaving the final words unspoken, but he saw the fear in her eyes, and her grip on the bedclothes tightened.

"Of course not!" he barked, offended. "You honestly think I

would harm you?"

"Well, you did just harm your door."

"Yes, and if you'd opened the bloody thing so I could explain myself to you I wouldn't have!"

"Don't shout at me, Sebastian, please," Julia said. "As you just mentioned, there is no longer a door separating us."

"I'm not shouting!"

"I dare say you are, you foul-tempered beast."

"I am not a beast!" But he was certainly shouting, she was right. With a ragged sigh he removed his jacket and set it on her dresser, then carried the armchair from the fireplace to her bedside. Taking a seat, he rubbed his jaw and sighed a second time before saying, "I know you're angry with me. I'd like a chance to explain, Julia. I never meant to hurt you."

"You didn't think discovering I was nothing more than a vehicle for your revenge would hurt?"

"You aren't."

"Of course I am. I asked you if it was true and you said 'yes.' That's fairly clear." She frowned.

"That's not what I meant. What Suffolk said about Amelia, about my being engaged, that was true. And I won't lie to you and say I do not find it incredibly ironic that the first woman I am attracted to in years is promised to the man who destroyed my happiness and drove me from society. It's perhaps the most poetic and unbelievable twist of fate I've ever heard of." Sebastian tugged at his cravat, which was quite suddenly choking him, and finally elected to remove it. "The first time I kissed you, I didn't know who you were. Nor the second time. I wanted you without even knowing your name."

Her mouth relaxed a fraction, as did her grip on the bedclothes. "Alright," she said. "I'm listening."

"Thomas Howard and I knew each other, years ago, but we were more rivals than friends. We spent a great deal of time trying to best each other at all manner of exploits – boxing, gambling, raking. In an attempt to settle once and for all who was the better pugilist, he fractured my nose, but not before

I broke three of his fingers." He ran two fingers down the bridge of his nose, which was slightly crooked as a result of the encounter now described.

"I was at Almack's hoping to find a new mistress when I saw Amelia for the first time. At the risk of sounding like some bloody fop, I was instantly smitten. She wanted nothing to do with me at first; my reputation was less than pristine and though I was in line for the title, I was not a duke yet. Her father, the Marquis of Landsdowne, wasn't pleased that I'd taken an interest in his only child. I didn't care, I pursued her relentlessly. We both did.

"I don't know when Thomas first saw her, or when he began courting her. It may have been genuine interest on his part, or just another competition with me. I'm inclined to think it was the latter."

The chair was suddenly too confining, the room too warm. Sebastian stood, removed his undercoat, and began to pace the room. Julia had leaned forward listening to his tale. She'd allowed the bedclothes to slip to her waist, and the paper thin cotton shift she wore did little to hide her figure.

"At any rate," he continued, "she eventually allowed me to court her. I desired her in a physical sense, of course, but I had it in mind to make her my wife, and so I never attempted anything untoward. I didn't want to compromise her. I wanted to marry her."

"You loved her," Julia supplied.

"Yes, I did. I proposed in secret. I wanted my father's blessing before any public announcement was made, and with him due in Town the following month, Amelia and I agreed to wait for his arrival. Her father knew, and approved.

"One night, at one of Lady Winterton's musicales, I stepped onto the balcony to have a smoke, and rest my ears. Does she still have those things?"

Julia nodded.

"Are they still awful?"

She nodded again.

"Couples often sneak out to the balcony or the gardens to be alone, as I'm sure you know. I wouldn't have cared who was out there in the dark, or what they were doing, but I recognized her laugh. I found her in the garden with Thomas. At the time, she told me they'd only gone for a stroll, and they both protested that anything scandalous had occurred. I challenged Thomas to a duel in defense of her honor. Later that night, in my carriage as I escorted her home, she told me the truth. She'd been meeting him in secret for some time. He'd already compromised her, before my proposal.

"I lost the duel, and Thomas gave me this as a parting gift." He gestured to the scar across his jaw with a scowl. "What happened next you already know. Amelia called on me, begged my forgiveness, pleaded with me not to break our engagement. I called her a whore, and several things worse than that. The next morning I received two letters, one from my father summoning me to Foxwaith and the other from the Marquis informing me of Amelia's suicide. I left London within the hour, and I've never returned."

Sebastian dropped back into the chair and covered his face with his hand. Five years of pain, regret and guilt welled up within him. No way in hell would he cry in front of her, but his control was nearly at an end.

A rustle of fabric was followed by a small, cool hand on his cheek. "Sebastian," Julia said. He heard her shift position to kneel in front of him, and her other hand settled on his knee. "It wasn't your fault."

"If I had forgiven her, she'd still be alive."

"There's no way to know that." Her voice was soft and silky, it caressed him as her hands did. "It was she who wronged you, not the other way around. If you had forgiven her, married her, would you have been able to trust her? You would have been stuck in an unhappy marriage with an unfaithful wife. You would have been no more satisfied than you are now."

He let out a ragged breath and finally lifted his head to meet her gaze. There was nothing in it but compassion and perhaps

—he hardly dared to hope—love.

"For five years she's haunted me. But not anymore. I can't even conjure her face in my mind when I try. Now, I only see you."

•

Just as quickly as he'd shattered her hopes, he repaired them. The raw emotion in his voice convinced Julia of his sincerity, and his pain. He was right about the irony of their current situation; fate was not without a sense of humor, it seemed. After listening to his story, she couldn't blame Sebastian for wanting revenge, and she better understood his desire for privacy. He viewed himself as a monster, carried a guilt that wasn't his. An overwhelming urge to comfort him flooded her, and on a baser level, to touch him.

Giving in to impulse, Julia stood and pressed a kiss to his cheek. She settled onto his lap feeling bold, empowered. Instantly, he arms circled her waist and pulled her tight against him. Thomas' mocking words replayed within her mind. *You're thoroughly ruined, darling, whether he's touched you or not.* Loathe as she was to agree with anything the man said, it was most likely true. A young woman couldn't disappear for weeks and escape speculation about her virtue when she returned; and if Julia never went back to London, it didn't matter, anyway. When analyzed in that light, the course of action she was currently considering no longer seemed so reckless. There was nothing to lose, and everything to gain.

"Sebastian," she whispered, pressing her lips against his neck. He stiffened for a brief moment but then relaxed. "Take me to your room."

"What?" The surprise was evident in his voice.

"I can't sleep here, your Grace, I have no door."

He turned his head, brushing his mouth over hers. "There are other rooms, sweetheart."

"I know. I want to go to yours."

Sebastian groaned. "I won't take advantage of you."

"No," she agreed. "Tell me—" Her breath passed over the

shell of his ear and he shook, just the slightest bit. Ah, good, she had his attention. His hands tightened around her waist, and she continued, "What would the Sebastian of five years ago have done with a willing female in his arms?"

His caress drifted lower, skimming over her derrière. "We wouldn't be doing this much talking, that's for sure."

"I suggest we stop talking, then." Acting on instinct alone, she let her tongue dart out and trace the hard ridge of his jaw.

"Christ, Julia. I only have so much restraint."

She chuckled, noting with fascination that her voice had become low and throaty. Seductive. "I hope so. Thomas was right about one thing, you know. My reputation is in tatters no matter what. Why not make my ruination both pleasurable and on my own terms?"

"Am I forgiven then?"

"Hmm, not yet." Trailing her hands down his chest she let them settle just above the waistband of his breeches. He drew in a sharp breath and she smiled. Her attempt at seduction was clumsy, but so far effective. Whatever she had the urge to do, she did, and thus far he was enjoying it. For a virgin, she was apparently doing quite well. Good. "But you have all night."

•

That was all the convincing Sebastian's conscience required. His body had been sold on the idea from the moment she'd seated her lovely ass on his lap. With the way she was tracing delicate circles from his ear down his jaw line with her tongue, he was surprised he had any rational thinking left at all. Good god, this woman was a virgin? She had him more excited than the most experienced of whores, and both of them were still clothed — a circumstance he intended to rectify without delay.

He stood, bringing Julia with him in his arms (and feeling rather proud that he'd accomplished the maneuver without stumbling), and carried her down the hall and into his chambers, kicking the door open with a booted foot. For the first time in over a week, his valet was present, stoking the fire that blazed in the hearth.

"Your Grace," the young man straightened and, upon catching sight of the half-dressed woman in his master's arms, dropped the iron poker.

"That'll be all tonight, William," Sebastian said. "Shut the door as you leave."

William nodded and fairly ran from the room, letting the door click shut.

"My word, you do have a valet," Julia mused.

"On occasion." On days when the man wasn't too busy getting drunk in the stables and hiding to avoid work. But that was a topic for a time when he didn't have a nearly and soon to be naked woman in his arms.

"Oh."

He set her down and her tiny hands immediately set to work unfastening the buttons of his waistcoat. She must have sensed his surprise because her hands stilled and she peered up at him. "Have I done something wrong?" she asked.

"No, I'm simply not used to a woman undressing me," he explained, one hand coming up to caress her cheek, then slipping through her curls to pull free the pins that still remained, holding her hair up. It fell over his hand and tumbled down her shoulders in a cascade of black, like an onyx waterfall. Christ, she was beautiful.

"Is it wanton?" her voice was a whisper.

"No. Put that word out of your head, sweetheart. Nothing we're about to do is wanton or shameful. But if you've changed your mind, best tell me now before I lose the ability to control myself."

"I confess to being a bit nervous, but I haven't changed my mind." Offering him a shy smile she resumed her task of unbuttoning.

Thank heavens. He let out the breath he hadn't realized he was holding. If she'd said "stop" he might actually have cried. Sebastian shrugged out of his coat and shirt, then bent and removed his breeches. When her fingers moved to the waist of his breeches, he laid a hand on them, stopping her. "Not yet," he said.

He wasn't sure how much she knew of sexual intercourse, and didn't want to reveal that portion of his anatomy until he'd put her somewhat at ease. He'd been rock hard since she sat down in his lap. Besides, if she started touching him there, and given the way she was currently tracing one finger around his nipples, he guessed he'd shame himself on the spot. Perhaps five years of abstinence had been a mistake; his stamina was no doubt sorely diminished.

As he lifted her shift up over her head, he was embarrassed to note that his hands shook. Bloody hell, he was acting like a virgin himself! Pulling the thin garment over her head, he tossed it aside and took in the sight of her. She was flawless, as he'd known she would be. Her breasts he remembered well, high and firm with dusky tipped nipples, large enough to overfill his palms. Her figure was slender, but healthy; a narrow waist flared out to full hips and a slightly rounded stomach above slim, pale legs and a tuft of jet black hair at the apex of her thighs. Julia allowed his carnal inspection, standing with her hands clasped, watching him through lowered lashes.

Lifting her in his arms again he carried her to the bed and set her atop the velvet, red coverlet, then stretched out beside her, head propped up on one hand, the other resting on the swell of her belly. "Still nervous?" he asked, brushing a few errant curls from her face.

"Yes," she whispered. "You look as if you're going to devour me."

Oh, I am. "Close your eyes. Let me set you at ease."

Obediently, her eyelids fluttered closed and her mouth parted. Sebastian skimmed his hand up her stomach to settle over one breast, testing its' pliant weight against his palm. When his thumb brushed over the tip she let out a tiny muffled sound, something between a whimper and a moan. His mouth found hers and he allowed her taste to flood his senses, cinnamon and honey. She relaxed some under his ministrations and he dipped his head lower, drawing first one peak, then the other into his mouth. Her hands clutched his shoulders, and she sighed.

"That feels good," she mumbled.

"There are many ways a man can please a woman," Sebastian murmured against her neck. His male pride reveled in her candid reaction to his touch, and his breeches were now tight to the point of being painful. Intent on maximizing Julia's enjoyment, he did his best to ignore the discomfort.

"Show me." Her voice was husky and low with wanting.

His hand slid between her legs, fingers gliding through the wetness of her folds. "There is a spot here," he said, as he found the tiny nub at the apex of her thighs.

"Oh … my." She trembled.

"Do you feel how it makes you quiver?"

"Yes," she hissed.

"Do you like it?"

"Yes!"

"Good, because I'm not stopping any time soon. I do believe I'm past the point of stopping now."

"Good," she echoed dreamily. "Don't stop."

Bloody hell, his mind intoned for the twentieth time that night. It was becoming a mantra, and at this rate he wouldn't be surprised if he was monosyllabic by the time they were through. He'd known she was passionate from the way she responded to his kisses, but he'd never suspected she'd be so vocal about her enjoyment. Not that he was complaining, of course. His hand, now coated in her slickness, moved faster.

"Sebastian," she moaned as her thighs began to tremble. "I—"

"I know, sweetheart."

"I need … Sebastian!" her voice rose to a shriek, nails biting painfully into his shoulders.

"Shatter for me, love. Let yourself go." Easing one finger inside her passage he began to thrust in a gentle rhythm, mimicking the act a much larger portion of his anatomy would soon perform. Her tiny, mewling cries were a continuous chorus as he added a second finger.

He felt it the moment she climaxed, the rippling of her muscles ratcheting up his need even further. He continued to coax her through her orgasm until her trembles subsided. With a final, gliding caress he withdrew.

"That was ..." she panted, one blue eye cracking open to peer at him, followed by the other. Her lips turned upward in a smile and she regarded him with a mixture of satisfaction and awe.

"Just the beginning." He rained kisses upon her face and neck, then lower, over her breasts and down her stomach.

When Sebastian lowered his head between her thighs he expected her to gasp, or push him away as other well-bred ladies, even the ones not innocent in sex, always did. But she merely watched him through hooded eyes with a mixture of fascination and curiosity.

He teased her with his tongue in the same calculated way he'd used his fingers, bringing her to the brink of release for a second time. Her moans again grew louder, more insistent. Pushing first one finger, then two into her, he continued to prepare her for him as he pleasured her. Julia speared her fingers through his hair, clutching him tight against her heated core. Her back arched, thighs clenched as she climaxed. Though the ultimate test of his skill was yet to come, he was proud to note he hadn't lost the ability to please a woman.

Settling back at her side, he noticed her pensive expression. "What's wrong?"

"Oh, no, nothing is wrong. That was— I hardly know how to describe it. But you are still in your breeches and I feel somewhat guilty that you've yet to receive any enjoyment. Would you like me to ..." she paused, and her tongue darted out to lick her lips. "... to reciprocate?"

Bloody hell! "One of the differences between men and women when it comes to making love," he explained, choosing his words carefully, "is that while a woman can climax repeatedly, a man requires time to recover before being able to continue."

Julia frowned. "That hardly seems fair."

He pressed a kiss to her temple. "I assure you, love, I'm enjoying myself quite thoroughly."

"Will you remove your breeches now, anyway?" she asked, and to prove her point she hooked one finger beneath his waistband and tugged. "I may not know much about sexual intercourse, but I do know that eventually we must both be naked."

A marvelous suggestion. Sebastian stood and stripped off his breeches, kicking them to the corner and rejoined his companion, who was watching him with open fascination. If the sight of his erection disturbed her, she didn't show it. Skimming a palm along his length, he turned and settled his weight over hers. She brought her hands up to his shoulders and, without prompting spread her legs so that his groin came into contact with hers.

"I'm afraid this is going to hurt, love."

"It hasn't so far," she answered innocently. A slight upward push of her hips made him groan. *Bloody hell.*

"I have to break your barrier. It's only the first time, and only for a moment." He hoped, anyway. He'd never bedded a virgin before, but Alex had once, by accident, and Sebastian had been treated to all the details over a night of brandied lamentation. "I'll go slowly," he said.

She nodded. "Not too slowly, I hope."

No, there wasn't any chance of that. With one hand he guided himself into her, gritting his teeth as he fought the urge to plunge deep. She was warm and tight, perfect. He kept his progress leisurely and controlled, but with each gained inch it became harder to ignore the masculine need to possess her completely. Upon meeting resistance, he bent his head and kissed her, then pushed forward, breaking through her maidenhead until he'd hilted.

Julia whimpered against his mouth and her body tensed. Sebastian kissed her again, smoothing her forehead with gentle strokes of his fingers. After a few moments, she began to respond, returning his kiss with tentative sweeps of her tongue along his lips. Her thighs relaxed again, dropping apart.

Withdrawing almost entirely from her slick heat, he moaned, half in relief, half in need, before sliding home again. His pace was unhurried to start, but each time she voiced her satisfaction with a cry or moan, he thrust faster, harder. Quick learner that she was, it didn't take long before she was moving with him, rocking her hips in time with his movements.

Too soon the sensations built, driving him towards completion. He hovered at the brink for one heart-stopping moment before her muscles constricted, and the rippling of her climax began. Releasing a strangled cry he tumbled with her into the abyss, and lost control.

It took several long moments to regain some semblance of motor function. Breathing ragged, he managed to roll onto his back, pulling her with him. She settled against his chest, with a soft sigh. It occurred to him that he should have taken precautions against the risk of pregnancy, but she'd felt too good, too right. If she happened to get with child, well … that was something they'd handle together. He had no regrets.

"Sebastian?" Julia spoke up a time later, still nestled against his side.

"Hmm?"

"Do two women really … I mean, can they?"

"Yes," he replied. "Some prefer the company of other women to that of a man."

"How?"

"Well," he paused, choosing his words carefully. "You derived pleasure from my fingers and tongue, didn't you? My male anatomy wasn't involved in that."

"Yes …" she said, followed by a quiet, "Oh. I see."

He pulled her closer.

"Would you want to watch me with another woman?" Julia asked.

"No." He shook his head. "I'm far too selfish. I want your moans to be only for me, caused only by me."

"What about two men?"

"Some do."

"I don't believe I'd want to watch you with another man," she buried her head against his shoulder. "I don't think I'd like it."

He chuckled. "I'm grateful for that." For the first time in five years he was content. "So, am I forgiven now?"

She yawned. "Oh yes, most thoroughly."

Satisfied, he gave into the pull of sleep, with Julia snug in his arms. The last thing he heard before drifting to sleep was her soft voice.

"I love you."

Chapter Eight

Waking the next morning wrapped tight in the circle of Sebastian's arms, Julia was happy. No, more than that, she was free. She'd done the one thing all well-bred English ladies were taught from an early age to never, ever do—she'd given her virtue to a man not her husband. Despite having prepared for it, the remorse and shame were absent. She didn't regret her decision at all, truth be told. As a woman, she owned little, and controlled even less. But her virginity was hers to give to a man of her choosing, no matter what her father or Aunt Margaret said. She'd chosen Sebastian, and no matter what happened next, she'd never be sorry for it.

Beyond the emotional attachment she had for the Duke, she couldn't deny the other reason she had no regrets. Quite simply, she'd enjoyed every moment. She'd possessed very little prior knowledge of carnal acts, and in fact hadn't been entirely certain what the deed entailed. With her mother passing when Julia was still too young to learn about male-female relations, her spinster of an aunt and dowdy friends were the only ones to ever offer insight. The ladies had never given her any indication that she'd take pleasure in sex at all, and they certainly hadn't explained, or possibly known, just how many things a tongue could do. She vowed that when it was her turn to school young debutantes she would not follow in Aunt Margaret's footsteps. No, she'd never dole out horror stories to young women when she was in her dotage, to be sure.

Julia had gained a notion the experience would be pleasurable from how much she enjoyed Sebastian's kisses, but heavens, never in a million years could she have guessed it would be like that. True, it had hurt for one brief moment, just as he'd said it would, but with so much pleasure before and after, it hardly seemed little more than a nuisance. Last night had been, in a word, perfect.

It had been so perfect, in fact, that for a moment upon waking Julia had thought it all a dream. But no, the very real, very naked man beside her, the faint soreness between her legs and the slick fluid that coated her thighs gave testimony to the fact that not a single, sinful detail had been imagined.

As if on cue, the duke stirred and his embrace constricted, pulling her tightly against him until she was almost straddling his muscular form. "Good morning" died on her lips as she noted that his breathing was still slow and regular, interspersed with the occasional soft snore. Heavens, this was awkward. Julia tried to wriggle free without waking him, but those sculpted arms of his were apparently for more than her admiration. She was trapped astride a naked, sleeping man.

But wait. Not every part of him was asleep, she realized, identifying the rigid length nestled against the folds of her sex. Testing her range of motion, she rocked her hips the smallest bit. Hmm … She repeated the gesture again. And again. Surely this was wanton behavior. She did it again.

"Bloody …" Sebastian murmured and his eyes flew open.

"Oh," she said as casually as she could manage, "good morning."

"What a clever way to wake me up."

She flushed. "That was not my goal. I, uh, was trapped up here, and searching for a method of escape."

He grinned. "Is that so? Well, my profuse apologies for holding you captive, darling. You are free to go." Releasing her, he laced his fingers behind his head.

She remained in place. Sebastian lifted one eyebrow, and his grin widened. "I never said it was an unpleasant trap,"

Julia ventured.

His other eyebrow rose to join the former. "As a gentleman, first and foremost, I must always see to my lady's comfort. Is there a way, do you think, I could make things even more pleasant?"

Good question, and while she wasn't entirely sure how to answer it, she did like his implications. "A gentleman," she replied, "should see to his lady without the necessity of her direction. It should be a natural, instinctual inclination on his part."

"But," Sebastian countered, bringing one hand up to trace the line of her collar bone, "a gentleman may not always know precisely what a lady wishes. I propose a compromise: I will employ my instincts, but you must provide me with critique."

"Very well."

"Splendid. Now," he took her waist between his hands and urged her back until she was in a sitting position. "How's this?"

She cocked her head and thought a moment. "Neither better nor worse."

"I see. And this?" Both palms slid up to cover her breasts. An upward thrust of his hips caused a delicious friction as he made contact with the place between her legs he'd shown her last night.

Julia moaned. "A marked improvement."

"Wonderful. Though I believe I can improve even more."

"Mmm?"

Strong hands lifted her upward and she felt the tip of his erection nudging at her folds. With excruciating patience, Sebastian eased her down until she was again seated in her former position, with one major difference. She felt impossibly full, and from this angle he seemed even larger than he had before, if that were possible. "Does this help?"

Her attempt at an articulate response came out as something between a moan and a sob. Yes, it helped a great deal, but she needed more. She recalled the way he'd thrust his hips and stirred the most exquisite sensations, but their positions were reversed at present. Surely he didn't expect her to …

"Move," he instructed, and she was pleased to note he too was having difficulty with coherent conversation. "Like before."

So he did expect her to. Bracing her palms flat on his chest she rocked her hips forward, and then back. Oh yes, that did feel good. Sebastian's hands returned to her breasts, tugging at the hard beads of her nipples. She sighed. It didn't take long for her to establish a rhythm, timid to start, then bolder as her confidence, and the pleasure, grew.

One of his hands left her breasts and Julia opened her mouth to protest. He silenced her by brushing his thumb through the curls of her sex, finding that sensitive spot again.

That wonderful thing was going to happen again. What had he called it? Oh, to hell with technical terms. Gripping her waist, Sebastian thrust upward into her once, twice, and then she was tumbling back into the abyss. She thought, for a moment, that she might die of pleasure. Her back arched as wave after wave of sensation washed over her. Julia was dimly aware of him shouting her name, his arms pulling her down against his body. She collapsed with a contended sigh, the uneven rise and fall of his chest matching her own ragged breath. His heartbeat thumped against her ear, strong and sure, reassuring.

"Sebastian?"

"Yes, love?"

"We're back to where we started." Save the light sheen of sweat and his length still buried inside her, she was in the same position as before.

"So we are."

"At this rate we'll never get up today."

"You'll hear no complaints from me," he replied. "Spending the day in bed with you sounds like a perfect plan."

•

While the pair did not, in fact, spend all day in bed, it was well into the afternoon before they parted to bathe, dress, and reunite downstairs. Had it not been for his grumbling stomach, and steadily increasing concern for Julia's comfort, Sebastian would have been more than happy to spend the next few days —hell, the next week doing nothing but make love.

Julia had proven to be more than passionate, the woman was insatiable. He'd created a monster. A stunningly beautiful, eager to please monster. She hadn't balked at a single thing they'd done, or worried about being "proper," one of those ton directives he'd always hated, even before his exile. Their lovemaking had been varied, slow and gentle one time, hard and fast the next. He still wasn't confident enough in his self-control to allow her to reciprocate his oral ministrations, but she'd asked. Twice. Just thinking about it was enough to have him painfully hard, again.

Sebastian had felt a pang of guilt when they'd finally climbed out of bed and he saw the small dark stain on his bed sheet. True, she'd been the instigator and at least so far showed no signs of remorse, but the fact remained that he had ruined her. There was also the very real possibility of her being with child. He'd bedded her more than half a dozen times in the last twelve hours, and not once had he taken any measure of care to avoid impregnation. If she left him …

Bloody hell, he didn't like that thought. He didn't want her anywhere but at Foxwaith, with him. He certainly didn't want her with anyone else. The idea of Julia with another man turned his stomach. No, she was his. He recalled her sleepy, whispered words from the night before. She'd said she loved him. Whether it had been truth, or a spontaneous admission spurred by lust, he couldn't be sure … but it had felt good to hear. Amelia had never said it.

You could always marry her, his conscience prodded. Get the special license now and there'll be no worry about a seven month child at all. Of course eyebrows would still rise if she gave birth nine months after their nuptials, but being secluded in Lincolnshire there was no reason for the ton to even know precise dates.

He didn't give a damn about his own reputation, but it wasn't his in danger, anyway. It was Julia's, and though she did not, now, seem to have any interest in London society, perhaps she would change her mind on that front. He'd never go back, but she could visit Catherine, or that dowdy aunt of hers.

Then again, simply marrying him would be a blow to her reputation. She'd be a duchess, and so the ton would not give her the cut direct, but if they all thought she'd wed a diseased, disfigured madman, well … she wouldn't get many invites to tea. Damn. Things were only getting more complicated, not less.

Sebastian resolved to stop worrying about it, at least for now. No need to give himself a headache mulling over "what ifs" and "maybes," not after the best sex of his life. There would be time to figure things out later. At the moment, he needed sustenance. He should probably spend an hour or two in his study, finishing off the stack of correspondence that had been abandoned yesterday afternoon, but he wasn't in the mindset to go through bills and accounting today. They could wait. His growling stomach couldn't.

Wandering into the kitchen, he strode toward his housekeeper who stood by the hearth brewing tea. Judging from the expression on her face, partially bemused, partially furious—she knew exactly what he had been up to.

"Good morning, my dear Mrs. Holland," he said, flashing a boyish grin and giving her a peck on the cheek.

"Don't you 'dear Mrs. Holland' me, your Grace," she scolded. "I should be furious with you."

"Should be?" Cocking an eyebrow he took a seat at the kitchen table. He rarely ate in here anymore, though as a young man he often spent hours at this table, simply wanting to be close to the woman who had served as his mother for most of his life.

"I told you to leave that child alone last night." She frowned at him, pouring two cups of tea and depositing them on the table. Grabbing a plate of biscuits from the counter she set them down and took a seat herself. "Not only did you ignore my advice, you went and ... well, you know what you did. And I know, too. For one thing, I may be old but my hearing is perfectly fine, and for another, that valet of yours couldn't make it to the kitchen any faster to spread the news she was in your room."

No surprise there. Neither he nor Julia had bothered being quiet last night. Or this morning. Or this afternoon. It was his house, after all, and there was no danger of his staff gossiping with anyone but each other. "But you're not furious with me, are you?" He took a sip of his tea. Ugh. He knew all Englishmen were supposed to favor the beverage, but in his opinion the bitter liquid was barely tolerable without a dash or two of brandy.

The older woman popped a biscuit into her mouth and sighed. "No, I'm not. Truth be told I'm pleased to finally see you happy again. Besides, anyone who saw the way you two tortured each other knew it was only a matter of time. It's how you handle things from this point that'll determine if you stay in my good graces."

"What do you mean?"

She clicked her tongue. "You know perfectly well what I mean."

He did, too. But how could he explain his ambivalence about the married state? How can you get past it? That was the better question, really.

Soft footsteps down the back stairs broke into his thoughts. A moment later, Julia entered the kitchen, clad in a burgundy day gown, hair pulled back in a simply coif at the base of her neck. The tops of her creamy breasts swelled above the square lace-trimmed neckline. An image of her nude and supine beneath him flashed through his mind and that perpetually eager portion of him leapt to attention with an almost painful throb. Blast, was he doomed to spend the rest of his life hard as a rock? This voracious attraction to her was supposed to get better now that he'd slaked his lust, not worse!

"Oh," she remarked upon seeing him. "Forgive me for intruding."

Mrs. Holland stood and gestured to the chair she'd just emptied. "You're not intruding at all, dear, have a seat. Would you like some tea? Or would you prefer to take it in the drawing room? How about a bite to eat, you must be famished." With the last she shot Sebastian a stern look. Not waiting for a reply, she began preparing another cup of tea, her back turned to the couple.

He couldn't help himself. Leaning forward in his chair he reached across the table and trailed two fingers along her collarbone before dropping them lower, tracing the neckline of her gown. Julia clamped one hand over her mouth to muffle a startled gasp, and used the other to smack his knuckles. She looked frantically at Mrs. Holland, whose back was still turned. Sebastian affixed his best wounded look, and withdrew.

"Temptress," he mouthed over the rim of his teacup and winked.

"Lecher!" she whispered back. An appropriate description of him at the moment, but from the smile she offered, he knew she wasn't angry.

"What was that, dear?" Mrs. Holland carried a cup of tea to the table for Julia, and set down a second plate of food, this one loaded with biscuits and scones.

"Oh, nothing," Julia flushed.

"Humph. I know perfectly well you two are making moon eyes at each other behind my back. No need to hide it. This is a kitchen, not some stuffy crushed ballroom where a young couple has to conceal their affection."

Sebastian laughed. His guest looked utterly mortified. "You're embarrassing the lady," he said.

"I see that. You should know by now, child, that none of that foolish frippery is required here. No hiding behind your fan and all the nonsensical rules of female behavior one must employ during the London season." She rolled her eyes.

"I do find myself more comfortable here at Foxwaith, but London wasn't so bad before my father tried to force me into marriage."

"If you say so, but I can't imagine it's changed much since my days," Mrs. Holland remarked.

"What do you mean?" Julia asked, lifting a scone to her lips.

The older woman shrugged. "I had a season myself, when I was a girl."

"What?" Sebastian hadn't intended to shout, but her statement shocked him. Across the table, Julia had dropped her scone and was gaping at them both.

Mrs. Holland shrugged again, and took a seat next to him. "My father was the third son of a Viscount. I had a season, spent time with my mother prowling the marriage mart. Pray don't shout at me again, your Grace, and my lady, close your mouth before you catch a fly."

There was a click as his companion's jaw snapped closed. "Mrs. Holland, why have you never told me this before?" he asked.

"There was never any point. Your father knew. He knew me back when I was Miss Whitten. I don't often talk about the past."

"But how is it that you ended up—I mean, that is to say, how did you come to be here?" Julia asked.

"You mean how did I go from socializing with the nobility to serving it?" She sighed and set her cup on the table. "Near the end of my first and only, as it happened, season, I met a young man, fell in love, and married him, much to my father's dismay. He was of the gentry, the eldest son of a wealthy merchant from the Colonies. I didn't care about a title, never had. I didn't care about the money, either, but my father always lamented the circumstances of his own birth. John's father wasn't pleased with the match either; he'd wanted his son to marry a woman higher up the social ladder than I, the daughter of an earl, or a marquis. But we were happy, we didn't care what our fathers thought.

"Within a year I was with child. We decided to quit London and go to John's home in the country until the baby came. There was an accident on the road, the carriage overturned." She paused and shut her eyes for a moment. When she opened them, they were moist. "John was killed. I lost the baby, and the physician informed me I wouldn't be able to have any children after that. My father turned me away for disobeying him. John's father blamed me for his son's death. I heard from a friend that the new Duchess of Rutland was pregnant, and in need of a nurse. I think your father was skeptical at first, Sebastian, but eventually he hired me.

"I was your nursemaid first, then your governess, and when Catherine came I cared for both of you. Then when Alexander was born and your mother died, I took much of your rearing into my own hands. Your father loved you all very much, as you know, but men ... well, they aren't always the best with children."

Sebastian nodded. His father hadn't been a very patient man, at least not when three young children were tearing through his study, building forts out of his accounting ledgers, and eating his correspondence (Alex had developed a taste for paper at an early age). As for his housekeeper's past, he'd had no idea. In truth, he'd never thought to ask. It wasn't that he didn't care; he'd told her many times he loved her like a mother, and he meant it, but she had always been simply Mrs. Holland to him. He couldn't picture her in some fancy ball gown batting her fan.

"When you were grown, all of you, the duke offered me a nice pension and a home near Grantham. Instead I asked if I could serve as head of household. I didn't want to leave here, and all of you, even if you no longer needed me. I guess I needed you."

"That's a miracle, with all we put you through."

She chuckled. "You put me through no more than any other children would have."

He had to disagree. "For the first twenty-seven years of my life I was a self-absorbed brat, and for the last five I've been a brooding tyrant."

"Oh, Sebastian, stop it." Reaching across the table she took his hand in hers and squeezed. "You were spoiled, by myself and your father. You were the heir to a dukedom, and you knew it. All young men who stand to inherit titles are a trifle arrogant. But you were a good lad, always. As for now, you've been a pain in my behind, but far from tyrannical. Besides, I've a feeling your days of gloom and doom have passed."

Indeed, it seemed they had.

"You don't miss it?" Julia spoke up.

"Miss what, dear? Town? The ton? Heavens, no. Never cared for all the featherheaded debs and their gossiping mothers, the fops and dandies, the rakes," Mrs. Holland said the last with a pointed glance in his direction. "I believe I ended up exactly where I was intended to be. Perhaps you have, too."

Julia's gaze flicked to Sebastian and she smiled. "Perhaps I have."

The trio continued to chat idly as they finished their small meal. When the cook appeared, grumbling about her schedule being disrupted when no one in the house wanted to eat normal meals, they took it as their cue to vacate the kitchen. Julia and Sebastian relocated to the front parlor, and Mrs. Holland bustled off toward the stairs, muttering about needing to find William, or any male willing to fix a smashed door.

"What's Catherine like?" Julia asked once they were settled, her with a book and him with the latest reports from his solicitor in London.

"She's something of a free spirit," he replied. "I suppose it comes from being around two rowdy brothers during her childhood. She was not pleased when our father arranged her marriage to the Earl of Whitmore, and I dare say she was downright overjoyed when he left her a widow two years later. Our father wanted her to come back home, or at least move in with Alex or I, but she refused, stating she wanted her independence."

Julia blinked. "Lady Whitmore is your sister? I had no idea."

"So you know her then. I thought you might, Catherine is quite the socialite. If she thinks a party might be a crush, she's sure to attend."

"Yes, she's always been very friendly to me. I saw her several places with Lord, but I assumed they were ..." She trailed off, blushing.

He laughed. Though it was true that nearly any woman was a potential conquest for his younger brother, he had no incestuous proclivities. Alexander would be mortified when he heard the conclusion Julia had drawn, which of course meant Sebastian couldn't wait to tell him. "Alex does his best to keep an eye on her. He's very protective of our sister."

"Speaking of your brother, I am surprised that Lord Cade didn't tell you my name," she remarked. "Unless he did, though I doubt it since you seemed so shocked when I finally told you the truth myself."

Sebastian froze. "What?"

"He must have recognized me. We were introduced once only briefly, but every time I encountered him after that he greeted me by name," she said. "Did he really not tell you?"

"And how many times was that, would you say?"

Julia shrugged. "At least a dozen. I last saw him the night before I ran away. In fact, we shared a dance."

He shook his head with a disbelieving snort. That sly bastard. He should have known Alex was setting him up. The taunting comments, the evasive answers, it was painfully obvious in retrospect. His younger brother never forgot a beautiful woman.

"Sebastian?"

"It seems," he answered finally, reaching over to take her hand and lifting it to his lips, "my brother thought to do me a favor."

"And did he?"

Pressing a kiss to her fingers he replied, "Yes. He certainly did." His heart seized at her warm smile and for a moment he thought it might burst.

Bloody hell. He was in love.

Chapter Nine

As it happened, Mrs. Holland was not able to locate Sebastian's frequently absent valet to fix Julia's bedroom door. Her belongings were moved into the Duchess' chambers, which were connected to Sebastian's rooms. In truth it didn't matter which room she was assigned; she spent her nights in his Grace's bed, and his arms. Each morning, she returned to her chambers to bathe and dress. The rooms were lavish, but tasteful, with rich purples and blues, and wood paneling of dark cherry. The large canopied bed, which Julia herself never slept in, had been a gift from Queen Anne to the first Duke of Rutland, upon his elevation from the title of earl.

It felt strange to be there, and more than a touch scandalous. She wasn't the Duchess of Rutland, after all, just plain Miss Deveraux, whose father was a joke amongst the ton.

A week had passed since their first night together. In the mornings, Sebastian was typically locked away in his study handling the tedious details of running a ducal estate. The afternoons he reserved for her. Whether it was riding around the estate, visiting the Bowers, or staying indoors reading, she was content to just be near him.

The sexual tension between them was palpable. She would often catch Sebastian watching her with pure, carnal interest. On more than one occasion when they were alone he would pull her close, whispering sinful promises of things he planned to do come nightfall. Several times when they were reading in the library or taking tea in the parlor, he would drop something at her feet—a letter, a spoon, whatever was handy—and take the opportunity to slide a hand under her skirts and tease her until she was half out of her mind.

Heavens, was she Sebastian's mistress? The label bothered her, but not because she was ashamed of their nocturnal activities. She disliked the term because it implied a carnal arrangement without emotional attachment, and over the course of a few short weeks she had become more than a trifle emotionally invested. Mistresses did not marry their lovers. And she did want to be his wife. She was hopelessly and completely in love with him. At least once a day she attempted to convince herself otherwise, but each time she looked at him her chest tightened, her breath caught.

Each night as she drifted to sleep within the comfort of his embrace she longed to blurt out those three words, but save that first evening together, she'd held her tongue. It was hard to tell how Sebastian felt about her. There was no denying he lusted for her, and the way he held her close as he slept, and kissed her forehead each morning in greeting implied he held some amount of affection for her, but she wasn't foolish enough to think he loved her in return. He'd loved once, and suffered for it.

Perhaps in time she could undo the damage Amelia had caused, but Julia knew she didn't have forever. Thomas Howard wouldn't be content to wait in London for her to change her mind, and there was no telling what the man would do when he came for her again. Would he bring her father?

Things could not continue this way indefinitely. What if she became pregnant? Despite her naiveté, Julia did know that repeated sexual activity would eventually result in conception. They'd made love numerous times each night for the last week. She could already be with child.

Mrs. Holland and Elizabeth seemed to have the same concern, because they'd both been watching her carefully, and Elizabeth had even asked when Julia was due for her monthly courses.

At present she was sitting at the vanity in her room while Elizabeth pinned her hair into a loose chignon. She was due to meet Sebastian for breakfast shortly. A second delivery of dresses from Madame Chloe had arrived two days before, and she was wearing a day gown of cream-colored muslin, with straight elbow-length sleeves, square neckline and high waist.

"It's good ye moved to this room, Miss," Elizabeth remarked, twisting a lock of Julia's hair and securing it in place against her nape.

"Why is that?"

"Well, because Miss Catherine will be usin' it tonight I imagine."

Julia's head snapped up. "Lady Whitmore is here?"

"Aye, just arrived a few moments ago. We didn't know she was comin' and Mrs. Holland is beside 'erself." A final set of pins and her curls were secure. "There we go."

Julia stood and smoothed her gown. "Thank you, Elizabeth."

"His Grace is in the front parlor with Lady Catherine."

She nodded and made her way downstairs to the aforementioned room. Julia inhaled a deep breath and rapped her knuckles against the door twice before pushing it open and stepping into the room.

"Good morning," Sebastian greeted her with a smile, leaving his spot by the fireplace to come to her side. "Did Elizabeth tell you about our guest?"

Our guest. He said it like she belonged here. "She did."

"This is my sister, Catherine." The woman sitting at the piano forte was indeed familiar to her as Lady Whitmore. Dirty blonde hair a similar color as her brothers, and the same striking green eyes, Julia was surprised she'd never noticed the resemblance before. "Catherine, I believe you know Miss Deveraux already."

"Lady Whitmore, so nice to see you again," Julia remarked.

"Heavens, Miss Deveraux, it is you!" Lady Whitmore

exclaimed, rushing forward to grasp her hands with a familiar smile. "I suspected as much, since you have been so mysteriously absent of late."

"Has there been much gossip?" Not that she cared, of course. Oh bother, yes she did.

Catherine shrugged and laughed. "La, you know how the ton is. There were whispers for a day or two, before your father informed Lady Marbury that you were sick, and had retired to the country until your health improved."

"And that was sufficient to silence the gossip?" Typically, such excuses only resulted in more tongue wagging, not less.

"Well, no," the other woman admitted. "But fortunately for you, Lord Anderson's daughter created quite the scandal later that same night. She broke her engagement to the Marquis of Windsmere and ran off to Gretna Green with her father's valet. Your disappearance was summarily forgotten."

"Oh my word. How is Lord Anderson?" The old Baron was a frail waif-like man who seemed near death on his best of days. On the one occasion Julia had spoken to him, he'd droned on about his nerves and his gout for what had seemed like hours, until she'd made a sufficient excuse to get away.

"He fainted right to the ground in the middle of Lady Marbury's drawing room when his footman came rushing in to deliver the news. I'd never seen a grown man suffer an attack of the vapors before. Poor dear. They say he's taken to his bed and not left since."

"Isn't the Marquis of Windsmere in his seventies?" Sebastian spoke up. "I thought he was already married."

"He was," Catherine replied. "Widowed several years back. His first wife gave him no children, but apparently he hasn't lost hope of siring an heir. He was quite frank about that being the reason for his marriage to Miss Anderson."

"Good God," he made a face. "No wonder the poor gel ran for the hills. Granted, I wouldn't have been surprised if the old man kicked up his heels halfway through their wedding night, in flagrante delicto."

"Sebastian!" the women exclaimed in unison.

"Be honest, ladies, both of you were thinking it." He leveled a knowing look at each of them in turn. "I've heard worse things from your lips. The both of you. Women!"

Catherine inclined her head toward Julia and whispered, "At times I miss my brother in London. At others, I'm so very glad he doesn't venture into public."

"You should have heard him at Madame Chloe's."

"Oh, those two are a horrible pair! If I didn't know better, I'd wonder if my brother wasn't raised by wolves."

"Enough, my dears. I'm hungry, and it's far too early for my ego to be completely destroyed." Taking her arm, Sebastian led Julia to the table, seating her to his right, and Catherine to his left. The cook had outdone herself this morning upon hearing of Catherine's arrival, and the spread of food was enough to satisfy even the heartiest of gluttons.

Their conversation throughout breakfast consisted of inane topics like the weather, which had been unusually mild of late, the latest fashions, and Alex's new horse. Julia waited for the inevitable questions about her presence at Foxwaith, but they never came. Catherine was clearly aware of the goings on in Town, so she must have known of the engagement with Suffolk. Either she already knew the situation, from one of her brothers, or she was too polite to broach the subject. Regardless of the reason, Julia was more than happy to avoid the subject. Having to explain to the Dowager Countess of Whitmore just what she had been doing with the woman's brother, who himself happened to be a duke. Well, the mere thought of it was enough to make her queasy.

"I propose an outing today," Sebastian announced, spearing a bit of his eggs en cocotte with his fork.

"That sounds delightful!" Catherine exclaimed. "Where shall we go?"

"I leave that to you, my dears," he replied.

"Miss Deveraux? Any preference?"

Julia considered it a moment. She didn't know of any

destinations in the area other than Grantham and the Bowers' residence. "I'm not the best person to choose, Lady Whitmore, with such limited familiarity of Lincolnshire."

"Hmm … We could go to the modiste. I need a new dress or five."

Their host snorted. "Catherine, shall I state out loud in front of my guest how far over your allowance you were last month? All of it spent on dresses?"

Catherine pouted. "Well, I don't need them, per se. But having a new gown for the theater next week would be a wonderful charity on your part, darling brother. And a new hat to match, of course."

"Between your rapidly growing wardrobe and Alex's new stallion, I find myself short on charity. Annie told Mrs. Holland this morning that you don't even wear half of your dresses before you are out purchasing new ones."

She harrumphed and pushed a square of ham around her plate. "That wasn't very sporting of her."

"How about we visit the Bowers?" Sebastian asked. "You haven't seen them in a while, and Mary will no doubt be dying to hear all the sordid details of London."

"Little Mary? What interest does she have with Town?"

He laughed. "She's fascinated. Has it in her head she wants a season. She grilled poor Julia to no end the other day about fashion and gossip."

"Really?" Catherine perked up. "Would John let her have a season do you think? I could chaperone her I'm sure. In fact, I imagine that would be quite fun."

"She's only six."

"Well, in a few years then." Her blonde curls shimmered in the morning sunlight as she shook her head. "But yes, let's visit them. That sounds like a lark."

"Julia?" Sebastian prompted.

"Yes, I quite like the Bowers." She was pleased by the suggestion, their last visit had been enjoyable. With any luck, Mary would refrain from her talk of weddings and babies in front of Sebastian's sister. But if not, well, the Countess seemed easy going enough.

"Splendid. To the valley it is. I assume you both must change into outfits more suited to riding. I'll have William tell Peter to saddles the horses for us. Shall we meet back here in an hour?"

The women agreed, and the small party disbanded to prepare for a day of riding and socializing. Julia returned to her rooms and, with Elizabeth's help, changed into her green riding habit. Her hair was pinned up in a loose chignon beneath her bonnet. A light dusting of face powder, a dab of alkanet colored blush across the apples of her cheeks, and a smear of Rose Lip Salve along her lips brightened her features.

Checking the clock upon the mantle, she saw that she'd managed to change in record time. She headed back down to the parlor room, intent on surprising Sebastian, who had been teasing her daily about the extensive rigors of the female routine.

The door was ajar, and she could hear Lady Whitmore's voice drifting through the foyer. "I'm pleased that you've chosen to rejoin the living, Sebastian, but…not even Alexander would do something this reckless. What were you thinking?"

There was a pause, followed by Sebastian's deep baritone, "I wasn't thinking, per se. I acted on impulse. It was, perhaps, a mistake."

Julia didn't need to hear any more. Backing away as quietly as she could, she turned and fled to her room. Her breath came in ragged gasps, tears building behind her eyes. She was not prone to the vapors, but would welcome unconsciousness if it would stop the awful pain in her chest. Who knew that a broken heart could be felt so literally? First, she locked the connecting door that led to his bedchambers. Then, sinking onto the bed, she buried her face within the pillows and cried.

•

Catherine had changed outfits in record time. His sister was never one to hurry when the adornment of her person was in question, and Sebastian suspected her motivation now was so that she might interrogate him about the recent developments in his life. She was far too polite to ask her questions in his guest's presence, but he'd known as soon as they were alone, she would be relentless. Sure enough, she'd barely taken a seat before she started. "I'm pleased that you've chosen to rejoin the living, Sebastian, but ..." she shook her head, "not even Alexander would do something this reckless. What were you thinking?"

What indeed? He'd been asking himself the same question all week. The answer, of course, was that he'd let a part of his anatomy not prone to logic or reason make the choices. "I wasn't thinking, per se. I acted on impulse. It was, perhaps, a mistake." He strode to the fireplace and braced a palm against the mantle, keeping his back to his sister. He wasn't ready to tell her his true feelings, not when he hadn't even told Julia yet. If Catherine saw his face, she'd know he was lying.

She laughed. "Oh, Sebastian, I know you better than that. I saw you looking at her before. You're in love."

He snorted. "Don't be ridiculous, Catherine."

"My goodness, you are!" She rose and moved to his side. "Look me in the eye and tell me you don't love her."

He couldn't. Damn her for knowing him so well.

"There's nothing wrong with being in love, big brother. She's an absolute treasure. I only hope your intentions are honorable."

"Of course they are!" he snapped. Having someone else ask the questions he'd been posing to himself all week was providing a great deal of clarity. "That's what I meant by a mistake. I should have asked for her hand a week ago. Before I took her virginity. "

"You do know she's betrothed to Thomas Howard." Catherine's voice had softened. "I heard talk of their engagement at the Winterton's soiree several weeks ago. I was quite perplexed that a blackguard like the Earl of Suffolk could procure himself an original like Miss Deveraux. We'd all heard the rumors of Viscount Herford's financial straits, but there were at least half a dozen other gents angling for her, including the Marquis of Kingsbury."

Kingsbury? That fop? Sebastian felt a pang of irrational jealousy. "Her father's arrangement, she wants nothing to do with the man. That's how she came to be here, in fact. She fled London and wound up unconscious in the roses."

His sister blinked. "And you rescued her? La, this is just like a novel! And you the hero who saves the damsel in distress! How romantic!"

Sebastian shook his head. How like his little sister to find this convoluted situation romantic. "It may be romantic, but it's also a bloody mess."

"Sebastian! Mind your tongue!"

"Where is Miss Deveraux?" he asked, changing the subject. Now was not the time for one of Catherine's lectures on manners and decorum. Those could go on for hours. He checked his watch. "She never takes this long to ready herself for a ride." It was true. He often teased her about taking hours to change her dress, but she was usually fairly quick about it.

"Shall I go check on her?"

Sebastian shook his head. "I will." Without waiting for his sister to protest he quit the room and headed up the main staircase. If Catherine got Julia alone, she'd undoubtedly try to glean more details about their unconventional relationship. He loved his sister, and knew she meant well, but he wouldn't subject his worst enemy to one of her grillings.

Her marriage to the Earl of Whitmore hadn't been a pleasant experience; their father had pushed for the match to strengthen a business deal between the two men. Whitmore, twenty years Catherine's senior had treated her pleasantly enough to start, but began openly flaunting his mistress at society functions a few short months after the marriage, making Sebastian's sister a laughing stock amongst the ton. She'd never admitted to any physical violence upon her person, but both Cade brothers suspected it was occurring. It had been a blessing when the blackguard was found in the East End near Whitechapel, throat cut in what appeared to be a robbery gone bad. Since his death Catherine had become a stickler for propriety, working to scrub away the stench of ton gossip and restore her reputation.

Sebastian's current actions had the potential harm not just Catherine's reputation as his sister, but Julia's. Lady Whitmore was protective of any young female who faced being thrown to the wolves of society; she knew all too well how tormenting it was.

He shook his head to chase away the negative thoughts. Julia's reputation would not be tarnished on his account. He needed to offer for her soon. And he would, but not with his sister scrutinizing his every move so closely.

"Julia?" he asked, tapping on her door. When she didn't answer, he tried the knob and, finding it unlocked, eased the door open a fraction. "Julia?"

Still no answer. He stepped into the room and made a quick survey. The curtains had been drawn and there were no candles lit, making it difficult to see anything in the dim, murky light trickling around the edges of the windows. The rustle of bed sheets drew his attention.

"Are you in bed, Julia?" Sebastian made his way over cautiously. She was there, on her side, face turned away from him.

"Mmmph."

"What's wrong, sweetheart?" He leaned over the bed and brushed his fingers along her shoulder.

She shuddered and turned her head into the pillow with a moan. "I … I feel a touch ill," she mumbled into the purple satin.

"What can I do?" he asked, placing a hand on her back. She shook again at his touch but he couldn't help it. He couldn't be this close and not touch her. It was a compulsion; quite possibly an obsession.

"Let me lie here a while."

"Alright." He didn't like feeling helpless. "I'll stay with

you."

"No." It came out as an anguished moan. "I'd prefer to be alone. Please. Go to the Bowers with Catherine, don't let me ruin the plan."

Sebastian was slightly hurt that she didn't want him to stay, but he nodded, fought the urge to push the issue. Bending, he pressed a kiss to her shoulder and left, letting the door click shut behind him.

Returning downstairs, he explained to his sister that they would be making the trip alone. He half expected her to march upstairs and assess the situation herself, but she only remarked that it was a shame and went with him to the stables, stopping in the kitchen to make sure Mrs. Holland checked on Julia when she had a moment. The pair mounted their horses and began to trek across the estate in silence. In fact, Catherine was being unusually quiet.

"Go ahead and say it," he said.

"Say what?"

"Whatever it is you're so intently pondering over there."

"I'm not pondering," she replied, though her expression indicated the exact opposite. Her brows were drawn together, lips pursed.

He shrugged and began counting the seconds in his head. Forty-eight, forty-nine …

"Not feeling well," Catherine mused with a frown. "Sebastian?"

"Hmm?"

"She's not often sick in the mornings, is she?"

"What? No, never. Why?" His head whipped around to regard his sister. She wasn't implying what he thought, was she?

"Is she expanding?"

He bought a few moments by feigning ignorance. "Expanding?"

"Pregnant, Sebastian. Should I be preparing for a joyous event in nine months time, one which will require a wedding decidedly sooner than that?"

Hell and blast. Damn. If he lied, she'd see through it as always. If he told the truth, he was in for a serious tongue lashing. He'd already more or less admitted to compromising his houseguest, but blatantly acknowledging he could have impregnated Viscount Hereford's virginal debutante daughter was something else entirely. "I already told you I intend to do the honorable thing, Catherine."

"Oh, heavens. Sebastian, I—"

"Leave it be."

"But—"

"Catherine, please."

"Sebastian, you have to consider, if she—"

He held up a hand. "Woman, you're going to drive me to bedlam. Then I won't be able to marry her."

His sister opened her mouth, glared at him, and then snapped her jaw shut with an exaggerated sigh.

Ah, blessed silence. He gave her five minutes before she started up again. He planned to enjoy them. One, two, three…

"Sebastian, that reminds me. Why on Earth did you replace my door?"

•

Julia wasn't sure how long she laid there, in the dark. She cried herself to sleep, and when she woke again, her head was pounding, eyes swollen and dry. She felt numb. Neither angry nor miserable. She supposed, in a way, she'd been expecting this.

There was only one thing to do, now. It was clear she'd overstayed her welcome.

Part of her desperately wanted to stay and confront him, to reveal just how much he'd hurt her. But she knew that if she did, he would woo her into forgiving him. One kiss was all it would take. Men had a habit of charming women into submission long enough to get what they wanted. Julia had witnessed firsthand her father's manipulation of her mother. Suffolk had nearly snared her, and now Sebastian had done it.

Of course he did not wish to marry her! What a fool she'd been to even hope. He'd made his thoughts on the matrimonial state perfectly clear a number of times, through both action and words. And then there was the old adage Aunt Margaret was always reminding her of. What man would buy the cow when he could take the milk for free? She had behaved like a lightskirt, and now she was being treated like one. It served her right.

Her reputation was no doubt in tatters. Even if her father had somehow managed to fend off the rumors, there was still the fact that she had been ruined. Few blue-blooded men would want her now — even the most seasoned rake preferred a virgin in the marriage bed, and she lacked the duplicity to lure an unsuspecting gentleman in such a way.

There was Suffolk, though. As despicable as she found the man, she was technically already betrothed to him, and he'd made it rather clear upon his visit that he wasn't bothered by lack of purity. Perhaps the marriage would not be so horrible. She didn't love him, but he also did not love her. He would want to visit her bed at first, to secure himself an heir but once she'd done her duty in that regard, chances were good he'd grow bored of her. Go back to Lady Marbury or another of his mistresses and leave her alone. Yes, it could work. If she couldn't have Sebastian, and he'd made it clear she couldn't, then the Earl was as good as any other man. Her father would be pleased.

Julia would not be dissuaded again. When Sebastian returned, he wouldn't be able to stop her. She'd already be gone.

After donning a modest walking dress and packing the rest of her things in the same spare valise she'd nearly used a week before, she went off in search of Mrs. Holland. She was helping Cook in the kitchen, setting out bread to rise.

"Where are you going?" the old woman asked with alarm upon seeing her.

"London."

"Did your father finally send for you?"

Julia shook her head. "It's time I return."

"What has Sebastian done?"

"He hasn't done a thing." And that is precisely the problem.

"I see." Mrs. Holland wiped her hands on her apron. "And he knows you're leaving?"

"No. I've left a note in his study, he should get it when he returns."

"Then how will you get to town, dear?"

She sighed. "I was hoping you could talk to the coachman, have him take me to Grantham at least. I'll secure a hack from there."

The housekeeper eyed her critically. "I think you should wait and speak with his Grace. If you still wish to leave after that, you can ride with Catherine when she departs in a few days."

"That's not an option, I'm afraid. I realize I've put you in a difficult position, but I really cannot stay at Foxwaith any longer. My mind is firmly committed to departure, be it with your help, or on my father's horse bareback, without."

The silence stretched out between them, the younger woman waiting and hoping, while the older seemed to search for a persuasive response. It was a waste of time. At long last, Mrs. Holland shook her head and sighed. "I'll have Bobby take you to London, then. But you're making a mistake."

•

Julia was gone. Sebastian and his sister had returned to the manor just before sunset, to find a distraught Mrs. Holland waiting for them at the kitchen door, with red-rimmed eyes and mottled cheeks. Never in thirty-two years had he seen the old woman cry. She'd explained in halted, tear-filled detail how she'd had Bobby ready one of the carriages and take Julia to London. By the time she finished, Catherine was also crying, and he felt damn near tears himself.

He should have been angry with his head of household

for allowing it, but it was clear she hadn't much of a choice. Besides, he was too distraught to feel anger, or anything but a numbing emptiness. It was five years ago all over again. No, it was worse. Amelia's betrayal hadn't hurt as badly as this.

She couldn't be gone. He read the crumpled note the seventh time. He knew it by heart now. Her handwriting was feminine and refined, with smooth lines and soft curves.

> *Sebastian,*
>
> *Thank you for your hospitality, and for showing me the wisdom of my father's decision before I made an even greater mistake. I am returning to London to carry out my father's wishes. My future husband will no doubt reimburse you for any expenditures made on my behalf.*
>
> *-J*

He didn't understand. It was as simple as that, really. He hadn't a bloody clue what had happened to make her leave. Hadn't she been happy with him? Had he mistaken desperation for love?

At present he was seated by the fire in his study, a tumbler of brandy in one hand and Julia's letter in the other. There was a soft knock at the door and his sister padded over to him, taking the chair opposite. "I knew it was too good to be true," he muttered.

"Did you quarrel before we left this morning?"

"No." The liquor burned a path down his throat, settling painfully in his gut. He closed his eyes and welcomed the pain.

Catherine shook her head. "Something made her leave."

"Clearly I did."

"Do you love her, Sebastian?" she asked.

"You know I do."

"Yes, and you know what you must do to win her back."

"I can't do anything. She's gone."

His sister leaned forward and placed a hand on his arm.

"She may be gone, but you know where she is. Go after her."

"She's in London, Catherine. You know I can't go there."

"I know nothing of the kind. Those demons you've spent the last five years fighting aren't in town, Sebastian, they're here." She tapped his chest, and then stood. "I'm going back tomorrow morning. Come with me, or spend the rest of your life wishing you had."

Chapter Ten

*J*ulia sighed and smoothed the folds of her gown as she waited in the parlor for her fiancé to arrive. Her father was seated across from her with a glass of brandy in one hand and the day's newspaper in the other. His waistcoat was mis-buttoned and his cravat was askew, as usual. A thin lock of grey hair was combed over his mostly-bald pate, making the sharp sideburns that extended down to his chin look almost comical. He was not quite intoxicated, but would be by dinner. He always was.

She'd arrived back in Town the previous day. The Viscount been first relieved, then angry, then furious once he learned his precious stallion was still at Foxwaith Manor. She'd sat quietly, head down, as he rang a peal over her for close to an hour. Aunt Margaret had been present as well, standing at his side, wringing her hands and shaking her head.

His largest concern, aside from the return of his horse, was that Suffolk would still honor their engagement. The Earl had been sent word of her return last night, and had replied that he would call this afternoon. He was due to arrive shortly, and Julia was not looking forward to the impending conversation. To be honest, she wasn't looking forward to much of anything anymore. Everything had come full circle, and she was now back exactly where she'd started. No, that wasn't quite true. She'd had a glimpse of true happiness, for the first time. Things were worse.

Anders, their elderly, stiff butler appeared in the doorway as if on cue. "My lord, the Earl of Suffolk has arrived," he announced.

Her father folded the paper and set it aside before nodding. "Send him in, please."

When Thomas entered the room a few moments later, he had a glint of triumph in his eyes. He crossed the room in easy strides to stand before Julia, who had risen to receive him. "Our wayward dove has returned to the nest." He grasped her hand and raised it to his lips. She fought the urge to yank it away. "It's a relief to see you returned safe and sound, my dear."

"Yes," she mumbled.

"Lord Suffolk, good of you to come."

"You can relax, Hereford, I've no intention of crying off."

The old man let out a breath. "Thank you, my lord. You can be assured I've spoken with her thoroughly about her foolishness and she promises she is committed to the match."

Thomas shrugged. "I told you she'd come around to the idea."

"Father," Julia ventured, "I would like to speak with his lordship in private a moment, if you please." Well, she didn't really want to, but it was necessary. She'd promised herself she would be honest with her future husband about the current state of her purity, or lack thereof.

Hereford's red-rimmed eyes shifted from his daughter to the Earl nervously. No doubt he was afraid she'd beg the man to reconsider.

"Why don't you head to Whites, Hereford?" Thomas suggested. "I'll join you shortly, to celebrate the union of our families."

"No, father can't …" she began. He'd been banned from the gentleman's club at the start of the season, for failure to satisfy his debts.

"He can," her fiancé replied. "I stopped by on my way here and settled his accounts."

"You did?" father and daughter asked at the same time.

"Of course. Consider it a gesture of good faith from your

future son-in-law." Suffolk's gaze flicked to Julia and the message in his expression was clear. You can't back out now. I own you.

Fortunately for both men, she was thoroughly committed, in mind though not in heart. That would simply never happen. She felt a combination of relief and dread as her father fairly ran from the room and left her alone with the earl.

"So, what is it you would like to tell me, my darling?"

Julia's hands fidgeted with her gown. "Well, I—I thought you deserved to know that— It wouldn't be fair if I didn't tell you …"

Thomas lifted an eyebrow patiently. He was very handsome. Strong, defined features with dark brown hair and matching eyes, a full mouth and regal nose, a body that was lean, yet clearly muscled beneath the finely tailored-clothing. He looked like the quintessential English gentleman. So why did her stomach curdle every time their eyes met?

"I'm not a virgin."

He smiled. "Ah. Did the deed after all, did he?"

"Yes."

"I'm guessing he didn't offer for you afterwards?"

"No, he did not."

She'd hoped he wouldn't be angry, but she hadn't expected him to seem pleased! "Do you still think him a better man than me?"

Julia lowered head and sighed. "No, I don't. You have at least been honest with me. I hope that in our marriage we will have a clear understanding of our obligations, as well as the importance of discretion." She held her breath. The last bit had come out far more assertive than she'd intended.

"Naturally," Thomas agreed.

"Good. I imagine we will get along fine, then."

"So tell me," he said, crossing the room and laying a hand on her cheek. She fought the urge to shiver. "When did the glorious event take place?"

"Must we go into details, my lord? I'm already

humiliated."

He chuckled. "If I wanted details, sweets, I'd be asking questions of a different nature, like if you were on your back or on your knees. I simply want to know when it happened. Was it the night of my visit?"

She nodded but didn't lift her gaze. She felt sick.

"Ha!" he barked. "I knew it. That's perfect."

"It is?"

"Oh yes, love. Most definitely." He didn't elaborate, and she didn't ask. In truth, she didn't want to know. "Are you carrying his child?"

Her head snapped up. Was she? She didn't feel pregnant. How would she know? "I don't think so, but I confess I'm not sure how I would tell so soon."

"Have you had your monthly courses?"

She flushed. "My lord …"

He held up a hand. "If your courses are late, then you are most likely pregnant. If you've not yet come due, then it's too early to tell."

Oh. "I've not had them," she said, "but I'm not due for a few more days."

"Then we'll wait and see. If you are with child, we shall simply have to expedite our nuptials to avoid wagging tongues."

"You'd marry me and claim the child as your own?" That she certainly hadn't been expecting. It would be Sebastian's child claiming his earldom, after all.

"Absolutely," Thomas replied with a leer. "It would be quite satisfying in a number of ways, and Rutland would no doubt know the truth, even if we managed to fool the rest of the ton."

Dear God. Julia felt nauseous. She was going to marry a monster.

•

The first thing he noticed was the smell. London had always been a foul assault on the olfactory senses, but five years away from the fetor, immersed in the fresh air of the country, had apparently cleansed his palate so that, upon entering the city again, he couldn't help but gag. He'd ridden into Town on the black stallion that belonged to Julia's father, figuring the old Viscount would likely want the animal returned to him, and that it would be a good excuse to gain an audience with him, as well as his lovely daughter. And while being horseback had increased his exposure to the stench, at least it had prevented Catherine from seeing him almost cast up his accounts; he'd never have heard the end of it.

London. As a man of two and thirty and a duke no less, he hated to admit fear or anxiety of any sort, but he was afraid. Perhaps Catherine had been correct in her saying that the demons he'd spent so long running from were inside him and not this foul-smelling city, but riding through its cobbled streets brought up memories best left in the past, feelings best left buried. He'd never thought to return, ever. The place had nearly destroyed him once. It might succeed this time. Was she worth it?

Yes, she was. But could he win her back? His sister was optimistic, but he wasn't so sure. Hell, he didn't even know why he'd lost her in the first place. The last two days had been spent reliving every moment he'd spent with Julia. Every kiss, every word … Surely there was some clue hidden within it all. There had to be. To think she'd felt nothing for him when he was in love with her was too much to bear. She'd only said it once, but she had told him she loved him. Had she been lying? Her note was impossibly cryptic. Damn it, he was lost. Two days of brooding had not made the situation any clearer. Catherine was right, though, he would win her back, or die trying.

The entourage stopped at Rutland House, to deposit Sebastian and his belongings. The large town home in West London had long been the residence of the Dukes of Rutland. Sebastian himself had stayed there often in his younger years, but ironically hadn't set foot in the coveted property since his elevation to the title. He allowed Alex use of the property year round—better to have it occupied than sit empty collecting dust.

His brother seemed both amused and aggravated to have an unexpected houseguest, not to mention annoyed at having been roused from bed before late afternoon. He appeared at the top of the stairs, shirt untucked, breeches rumpled, just as Sebastian stepped into the foyer.

"Well, well," he said, raking a hand through his hair, which clearly hadn't seen a comb in some time. "What an early morning surprise."

"It's nearly two, Alexander, and hello to you too," Sebastian replied.

"Two, is it?" His brother grinned. "Well, time for a drink, then. Care to join me in my, or should I say your, study?"

With a nod, he followed Alex through the second door on the right. The study hadn't changed much, save the mountainous stacks of papers strewn across the desk and floor. That meticulous neatness Sebastian had gotten from his father apparently only passed to first sons. "My god, Alex, what is this mess?"

The younger man shrugged. "One accumulates many things in one's lifetime."

"Have you considered cleaning it?"

"I've considered it, yes. Done it, no. I'm assuming I'll have to clear out now, eh? Come to take back over?"

Sebastian snorted. "No, thank you. The study's yours, and I'll gladly sleep in one of the guest bedrooms."

"No need for that, the master suit is empty. I keep the same rooms I did before you went into hiding."

That was a surprise. "Why?"

"Always hoped that one day you'd come to your senses and remove your head from your arse." Alex poured two glasses of port, handed one to Sebastian, and lit up a cheroot. "Figured it would be over a woman, too."

"Congratulations, Nostradamus," Sebastian replied. He'd

prepared himself for some ribbing, but his patience was thin. He was exhausted from the journey, and that bloody stench had either followed him inside, or was clinging to his clothes, or both.

"Oh, come now, your Grace. No one is happier than I that you've decided to do your duty, thus removing the obligation from my weary shoulders." Alex settled into a chair by the far wall, and Sebastian followed suit, taking the seat next to him. "So, what prompted this visit to Town? Come to get the special license and speak to her father?"

"Not exactly, no. I wouldn't get your hopes up just yet."

"Why the bloody hell not?"

He sighed and rubbed at scar along his jaw. The damn thing had been throbbing nonstop for days. "I've come to try and speak with Julia."

"What's she doing here?"

"I don't know. She left Foxwaith two days ago and returned to London."

"Why?"

"I don't know that either. But I intend to find out."

Alex frowned. "She didn't tell you why she was leaving?"

"She didn't tell me she was leaving at all. I came home and found her gone. Apparently she has a mind to honor her engagement to Thomas Howard."

The frowned deepened to a scowl. Tossing the remnants of his cheroot into the fire, Alex said, "You'll have to intercept her then. Chances are she'll be at the Tilsdale's ball tomorrow night. Catherine made me promise to put in an appearance."

"I wasn't invited." Sebastian hadn't been invited to anything in years. He liked it that way.

"You don't need a bloody invitation, brother, you're the Duke of Rutland."

"That's true," he mused, "I am."

Alex grinned and stood. "Come hell or high water, Sebastian, I'm going to see you get your woman back. My own sanity depends upon it, not to mention my bachelorhood."

Chapter Eleven

*T*he ballroom was stifling. Lady Tilsdale, overjoyed that her party was a resounding success, flittered past where Julia stood beside her aunt, taking a break from the dancing and sipping a glass of punch. It was definitely a crush. Most of the ton was present, and there was a rumor that the Regent himself might make an appearance.

Julia didn't much care who was there. If Prince George arrived and asked her to waltz, it wouldn't be enough to raise her spirits. Thomas had accompanied her and Aunt Margaret tonight, saying it was necessary for her to appear in society once more before their engagement was officially announced.

He and the Viscount had staved off the rumors by telling friends that she had fallen ill, and gone to the country to recover. It made sense, and thus far the evening had gone well. Her dance card was nearly full, and not even the gossip mongers seemed suspicious of her absence. Thomas had shared the first dance with her, and then disappeared into the card room.

She was wearing one of the dresses Madame Chloe had made for her, at Thomas's insistence. It was a deep burgundy silk, with muslin trim and a daring neckline. Lady Tilsdale had complimented her on it at least four times already. Lord Marbury told her she was outshining all the other females in attendance. She was miserable.

Sebastian had once called London hell on Earth. His assessment didn't seem far off the mark. Had she stayed at Foxwaith, she would be in the library now, with a cup of tea and a novel, Sebastian sitting beside her with his own book and a glass of brandy. Occasionally he'd reach over and stroke her hair. It had been their evening ritual, a way to pass the time between dinner and bed.

Instead, here she was in this clogged, muggy ballroom being ogled by every rake, fop, and dandy in London. She'd been right to leave Sebastian, she knew. Why, then, did everything feel so wrong?

Lost in her own gloomy thoughts, she didn't notice their small party had increased in number to three until the newcomer spoke.

"Miss Deveraux, would you take a turn with me around the room?" Alex Cade extended his hand, gracing her aunt with one of his devastating smiles.

"I really shouldn't leave my Aunt," she began, knowing it was likely hopeless.

Margaret scoffed. "Oh hush, dear. I'll be just fine. Now, go." Aunt Margaret was incapable of taking a hint. "Off with you! And bring me a punch when you are through, it's impossible to avoid being parched in this room."

"You're not frightened of me, Miss Deveraux, are you?" Alex asked as he led her away.

"Of course not," she replied.

"The vultures are abundant tonight, and particularly hungry," he muttered with a disgusted shake of his head. He was right; half a dozen young debs and their matchmaking mamas watched the pair with narrowed eyes as they strolled around the perimeter of the ballroom. "My brother tells me you left Foxwaith rather suddenly," Alex commented, speaking in low tones to avoid being overheard.

"I could hardly afford to dally there any longer, Lord Cade, with my impending nuptials," Julia replied with equal calm, careful to keep her eyes on anything but her companion.

"Bollocks," he snorted, and Julia jerked at the expletive. "Something happened. Sebastian won't say what, either, but he was the most morose I'd ever seen him, and given his penchant for brooding, that's significant."

She bristled. Was he really bothered by her departure? Good. "That is not my problem."

"Oh, it's about to be," he countered cryptically.

They rounded the corner of the dance floor, past the wide double doors which led to the hallway of the home. The balcony doors were ahead, propped open to allow guests access to the veranda and gardens below. Several groups of men had gathered just inside, likely so that they might have an easy escape route should they require it.

One man in particular stood out. He was tall, towering over most of the other gentlemen nearby, and even with his back turned, his blond hair and broad shoulders left no doubt as to his identity. Julia's feet became leaden and she pulled her companion to an unexpected halt. It had to be some sort of hallucination, brought on by the heat. She'd been thinking of him all evening, her mind was playing tricks.

"I tried to warn you, sweeting."

"You see him?" If Alex saw him too, that meant he was real, after all.

"See him, hear him. He's been a pain in my side since yesterday morning when he arrived."

"Why is he here?" she asked in a panicked whisper.

"In the hopes you would be."

"But why is he in London at all?"

"Again," Alex replied, "because you are."

Rendered immobile by her traitorous legs, Julia did her best to remain composed as the man ahead of them turned and she caught sight of his face. It seemed so out of place to see Sebastian here, in a crowded room amidst the ton. Yet, there he was. And heavens, he looked good. He eyes swept across the crowd, searching for someone … her?

She felt a jolt of recognition along her nerve endings when he caught sight of her, the heat in his gaze reminiscent of their last carnal encounter. He strode toward them with determination, mouth set into that firm, hard line she'd become so familiar with. She was aware of his eyes sweeping down her curves, noted a faint flash of satisfaction when he recognized her dress as one he'd selected—and paid for. Heat pooled low in her belly. Would he whisk her onto the balcony and kiss her breathless? Surely they could slip away unnoticed if they were careful. No! She wouldn't be charmed by him again. She would not!

"Good evening, brother," Alex said smoothly. "Allow me to introduce you to Miss Julia Deveraux, Viscount Hereford's daughter. Julia, my brother, Sebastian, Duke of Rutland."

"Miss Deveraux," Sebastian murmured and bowed. "A pleasure." Without waiting for her to offer her hand, he took it, brushing his lips across the knuckles.

Julia let out a sign of relief. There could be no acceptable explanation for her knowing Sebastian when he'd been a recluse for the last five years. If he'd acted familiar with her in any way, it would have set tongues wagging. In her peripheral she could see a group of older ladies, all notorious gossips, watching them with open-mouthed interest. "Your Grace," she managed. *I do not find you handsome*, she repeated silently. *I do not find you handsome!*

At that moment, the music ended, signaling the close of one dance and the beginning of another. She saw the determination in Sebastian's gaze, and prayed silently that it would be the quadrille or the cotillion, something that would not put him so close to her. Her heart sank as she heard the beginning notes of the waltz.

"May I have this dance, Miss Deveraux?" Sebastian asked smoothly.

"My card is full, I'm afraid," she lied. "And I have promised to waltz with Lord Carrington next." *I do not find you handsome!*

"Ah, but Lord Carrington is already on the floor."

A quick scan revealed that he was. Damn. If only she'd picked someone else to use in her lie, someone not wearing a bright pink overcoat visible from half a mile away. "I will sit this one out, then," she began, but it was too late. He was already leading her to the center of the room, with a firm grip on her elbow. "I do not wish to speak to you," she hissed.

"Then don't. Just dance."

"And I do not find you handsome!" Oops. That bit she hadn't intended to say aloud.

"No?" He chuckled. "You wound me, and make my task more difficult."

They took a place in the middle of the floor. Sebastian took her right hand in his left, and settled his other hand on the small of her back. His muscles were taut and firm under her palm as it rested on his arm. He felt like home. "I've missed you," he whispered, keeping his voice low.

"You're holding me too close," she hissed.

"Not close enough by my estimation," he countered, and his fingers flexed against her back for emphasis.

"Stop that!"

"Why?"

"Because!"

His lips curled. "Where would you like me to put my hand, then? I can think of a few locations that would be much better."

"You cannot tempt me into forgiving you with that tongue of yours," she retorted. Too late, she realized the double entendre.

He flashed a wolfish grin and licked his lips. She recognized that look, it was the same one he wore when she was in his bed chamber. "Can I at least be permitted to try?"

"I will not be lured into your bed!" When his grin widened she added, "Again."

"My, my. You're just full unpleasantries, angel."

God, she couldn't stop staring at his mouth. It looked full, and soft, and she knew just what it felt like against her skin. She felt eyes on them, knew they were close to creating a scandal. "I do not find you handsome," she said again.

"You mentioned that."

"Stop looking at me that way."

"What way, sweetheart?"

He was infuriating. He was … perfect. She switched topics. "You swore you'd never set foot in London again."

"Things change."

"Like what?"

"Like me. You have changed me, Julia."

What was he playing at? She didn't understand. He hadn't wanted to make a commitment, and she'd saved him the trouble of telling her so. "Yes, back into the unrepentant rakehell you were before. Of all my lifelong accomplishments, this one makes me truly proud."

•

Sebastian flinched. Unrepentant rakehell? Where had that come from? "What do you mean by that?"

"You know exactly what I mean!"

Actually, he didn't have a damn clue. Bloody hell, it felt good to have her in his arms again, even if she didn't want to be there. He recognized her gown. It was one he'd purchased for her, the dark burgundy color he'd insisted upon. It had been a good choice; she looked radiant. Lord Carrington twirled past with his partner, and was not subtle about craning his neck to ogle Julia's cleavage. Sebastian bit back a snarl and fought the urge to punch the man. "You've changed your perfume," he commented against her ear.

"I have not."

Sebastian chuckled. "This is lavender, you usually wear rosewater."

"I hate rosewater," Julia stated with vehemence.

"You wore it every day in my presence."

"And I hate you as well, you blackguard."

"No, you don't," he replied, unfazed by her anger.

"Yes, I do."

Blast, this wasn't going well at all. "No," he said calmly, "you don't." He wanted to kiss her. The look on her face told him she would smack him if he tried. "Why did you leave me, Julia?" There, he'd said it.

"What point was there in staying?"

Ouch. She'd been spitting barbs at him from the moment he'd approached her, but this latest was particularly painful, for both his ego and his heart. "To be with me," he replied finally. "I thought it was what you wanted."

Her eyes were icy daggers as she scowled at him. "Oh yes, right. I should have stayed with you as your mistress until you were no longer entertained by our nocturnal activities. Then I could have returned to London a ruined spinster, or even better, with a duke's bastard in my belly. You've ferreted out my heart's desire exactly!"

"Mistress?" Sebastian frowned, taken aback. What in the hell had put that notion in her head? He'd never said he wanted her as a mistress. The idea was absurd. "I don't want you as my mistress, Julia. I was hoping for something more permanent and honorable … like my wife."

"Ha!" she exclaimed loudly. The couple closest to them, Lord Maxcomb and his wife, gave them a sharp look. Lady Maxcomb tried to steer her husband closer, no doubt in the hopes of overhearing some juicy morsel. Sebastian twirled Julia around in a circle and put as much distance between them and the old bloodhound as he could. Oh, he despised the ton.

"Please explain why you find that so incredulous," he murmured. He'd thought his admission would soften her anger at least a fraction. Then again, the whole conversation thus far had been a bloody disaster.

"You don't wish to marry me, or have a life with me. You don't love me, and don't want me to bear your children. So why would you want me as your wife?"

"That isn't true," he replied. Would the woman always think the worst of him from now on? He was baffled by her anger.

"It is true. Stop treating me like some bumble headed feather brain."

"What in the world has made you think so?"

"You have. You 'acted on impulse.' You called it a mistake."

She paused and pulled her bottom lip between her teeth, worrying it. For the first time her eyes softened, and he saw the raw hurt behind her anger. "I heard you."

Damn it to hell. So she overheard him talking to Catherine. Her sudden illness that morning, the way she shrank from his touch … Now it made sense. He was a bloody fool for not seeing it. "I'm a fool."

"In that regard, we agree."

"I don't deny saying it, Julia, but I didn't mean it." The music was slowing, the dance drawing to a close. He didn't have much time left, the second she had the opportunity she would bolt, he could see it in her eyes. "Give me another chance. Let me prove I'm genuine."

"No," she shook her head. "I'm engaged to the Earl of Suffolk."

"But you hate him. You ran away to avoid marrying him."

"And that was very stupid of me. You see, Thomas can't break my heart, Sebastian. You've already done it."

Pain lanced through his chest. He felt sick. She hated him, and worse, he deserved it. "Don't marry him because of what I've done, Julia, please. You've seen firsthand how cruel he is."

The music stopped. The pair came to a halt, and for a long moment, he didn't let her go. Julia regarded him with a frown and tugged her hand from his grasp. "His cruelty can never compare to yours, your Grace."

Before he could stop her, she turned and hurried off into the crowd. He sighed and turned to search for his brother. He needed a drink. Halfway to the balcony, where he expected his brother to be, a familiar face stepped into his path.

"Well, Rutland," Thomas Howard said with a smile, "it seems I've won. Again."

"Get out of my way before I strangle you with my cravat." Ah, but that would be satisfying. Seeing the bastard's face turn red while he gasped for breath.

"Now now, violence never solves anything," the Earl

replied. "We wouldn't want to mar that noble face of yours any further."

"I'd take great pleasure in rearranging yours."

His nemesis laughed. "I'd be more than happy to let you try a second time. But stay away from Miss Deveraux. She's mine."

"We'll see about that," Sebastian growled. "You haven't won anything yet."

•

"So," Thomas interrupted the silence, propping one booted foot on the seat beside her. They were in his carriage on the way home; he'd acquiesced to her request to leave almost immediately after she'd parted ways with Sebastian. "What did Rutland want?"

Julia sighed and rubbed her temples. She'd not enjoyed being with Sebastian tonight, things had been awkward, and the conversation unpleasant. But she disliked being away from him more. If only it was he sitting across from her now. Sheer force of will was all that kept her from falling into his arms and begging him to whisk her away. "It was only a dance. I tried to decline, but he persisted, and I could hardly give him the cut direct without raising a few eyebrows."

"I'm not angry that you danced with him, dove. If sharing his bed didn't bother me, why would a waltz?"

"Thomas, please!" She cast a worried glance at Aunt Margaret. The older woman's mouth was open, head dropped back, snoring softly. A thin line of drool ran from the corner of her mouth to her chin.

He snorted. "The old bat is sound asleep, and even if she weren't, she's deaf as a post. Napoleon could march his army through her bedroom and she wouldn't notice. Now, I want to know what he said to you."

"I'd rather not talk about it."

A chuckle this time. "What would you like to talk about then, my dear?"

"Anything else."

"How about our impending nuptials?" Leaning forward he placed a hand on her leg.

She fought back another sigh. "If you like."

"How about our wedding night?"

Lord, not this again. Every time he had her alone he delivered lascivious (and thoroughly detailed) promises of their marriage's consummation. She was no longer a blushing virgin, and understood perfectly well what he meant to do, but the thought of doing those things with him, or really any man except Sebastian, was revolting. "If you like."

His hand slid higher. "Come sit next to me."

"I can't, I'll wake Aunt Margaret."

"I doubt it. She really is a pathetic chaperone, much to my delight. Besides, if you won't tell me what you discussed with the Duke I'll be forced to assume the worst. Unless…"

"Unless?"

"Unless you prove to me you still intend to honor our engagement."

"I've already told you I do." Her stomach turned.

"Yes, but with Rutland in Town, and obviously pursuing you, I require more convincing. You must show me."

"How?" She curled her hands into fists in her lap.

"A kiss would suffice." When she made to protest his fingers circled around one of her wrists and gave a tug. "Just a kiss, my dear."

"Thomas …" Julia cast a desperate glance at her aunt. Please wake up! The old woman snored on. She'd get no relief from her so-called chaperone. She could continue to stall and pray they were close to home, or acquiesce and pray he kept his word. Besides, she'd have to do this and more eventually, anyway. Perhaps it wouldn't be so bad.

"One kiss." He tugged at her wrist again and this time she didn't fight him, allowing herself to be pulled across the carriage and into his lap.

"This is most improper," she said weakly.

"My kiss, my rules," he replied, releasing her arm and

bringing his hand up to caress her cheek. Strong fingers kneaded the muscles in her neck and, despite herself, she sighed. It was not entirely unpleasant if she closed her eyes and pretended it was someone else's touch. Like Sebastian's. Her lips parted slightly as she conjured his image.

The mouth that covered hers a moment later was most definitely not Sebastian's. Thomas' kiss was hard and demanding, almost painful; harsh, just like he was. Julia whimpered, and he took it as an invitation, pushing his tongue into her mouth, exploring and claiming. It was, in a word, disgusting.

Placing both palms against his chest she pushed as hard as she could in an effort to disengage from his embrace. He allowed her to pull back, but when she attempted to slide from his lap he held her firmly in place. "Just a single kiss, my lord, remember."

"Do you have any idea how much I want you, darling? At first, I was angry with you for being so coy but now I find myself enjoying the anticipation."

She did, actually. The hard bulge pressing against her leg was rather unmistakable. She shuddered. His grin indicated he mistook her revulsion for expectation. The carriage was slowing, and a glance out the window revealed they were pulling up to her townhouse. Thank God. "Patience, Thomas," she said, "you shall have me soon enough."

Unfortunately.

•

"What am I going to do? She wouldn't even speak to me," Sebastian raked a hand through his hair with a frustrated sigh. He and Alex had left the ball not long after Julia and headed to White's in the hope of having a drink or two in peace. Unfortunately, even tucking themselves in the farthest corner of the club behind a potted fern hadn't been sufficient; every gentleman who entered headed straight for them, eager to catch a glimpse of the mysterious Duke of Rutland. Before long they'd abandoned any attempt at being inconspicuous and had quit the place entirely. They were now safely ensconced in the parlor of Alex's townhome—or more appropriately, *his* townhome.

"Damn it, I'm the Duke of Rutland! She can't just—just ..." Couldn't what? He didn't know.

"You should have seen Suffolk's face when he emerged from the card room and found her in your arms. For a moment I wasn't sure if he was going to shoot the cat or go at you with a carving fork from the hors d'oeuvres table."

"He confronted me afterwards, tried to taunt me into a fight."

"The man's dicked in the nob," Alex said.

Sebastian tipped his head in agreement. "Doesn't help me get through to her any, unfortunately."

"I don't know what you did to run her off, Sebastian, but the woman is furious. You should have heard what she said when she saw you. Quite a shocking word for those delicate lips," Alex replied, lighting up a cheroot. "You have one advantage, though."

"And what's that?"

"She's in love with you."

Sebastian snorted. "It's hardly helping."

"You're going to have to court her, brother."

He suppressed a groan. He knew what the ton considered standard procedure for courting a young woman. He'd done it once before. Why couldn't she just hear him out, then forgive him? It was unfair to make this all so ... excruciating.

Alex took a drag from his cheroot and exhaled, the cloud of dingy grey smoke temporarily dulling the light of the fire before dispersing. "You could always trick her. Lure her into a compromising situation and ensure that you're caught. Then she'll be forced to marry you. Not the most subtle technique, I admit, but it would do."

"Alexander!"

"Well," the younger man shrugged. "As I said, it's not very subtle, but it's tried and true. Countless scheming debs and even a few desperate dandies have lured their quarry into parson's mousetrap. Hell, it's why I sleep with one eye open and never wander off alone with an unmarried female."

"You sound like a matchmaking mamma."

His brother rolled his eyes. "Lately I feel like one."

"Yes, you've been quite busy these last few weeks, haven't you?"

"Have I?"

"Claiming you didn't know who she was? Going out of your way to make me jealous? Yes, I dare say you've become rather astute at it. Catherine would be proud."

Alex chuckled. "I was wondering how long it would take you to figure that out. Of course I remembered her name. You think I'd forget a woman like that?"

"No, I don't," Sebastian replied, taking a sip of his brandy. "But at the time, I was too distracted to catch it."

"I'll tell you honestly, if she hadn't been a virgin—" Seeing the duke's expression turn murderous, he trailed off. "If I had to be leg shackled, I'd want someone like your Julia, and for more reasons than her delicious assets." Sebastian growled. Alex held up his hands in surrender. "Court her, woo her, compromise her if you must, brother, but whatever you decide, do it soon. I think she's just angry enough to do something foolish like marry that horse's ass."

Sebastian nodded. He knew she was. Since when had his brother become a paragon of sound advice? He never thought there'd come a day when Alex made sense.

"Besides," the younger Cade added, "I've decided I'd like a sister-in-law by the end of the Season. And perhaps a nephew by the end of the next. Then, at long last, blessed freedom will be mine."

Chapter Twelve

"The Duke of Rutland has come calling, my lord."

Julia coughed loudly as her tea went down the wrong way. Aunt Margaret gasped and gripped her chair as if she expected to succumb to the vapors any moment. Her father's coffee cup slipped from his hands and shattered against the corner of the table.

"Please tell him I am not home, Anders," she said. "Send him away."

The Viscount sputtered. "He's a duke, girl. I don't care what ridiculous feminine sensibility of yours he's offended, I will not give him the cut, and neither will you. Show him to the parlor, Anders."

The butler nodded and quit the room.

"My feminine sensibility, father? He nearly ruined my reputation!" *If only you knew how ruined I am.*

The man snorted. "He didn't kidnap you from your bedroom and force you out the door dressed in rags, nor did he make you steal my horse, nor did he inspire you to ride halfway across England bareback alone. No, if anything, he did your reputation a favor, and I'd like to thank him for it."

Julia bit her tongue. Sebastian most certain had not done her reputation any favors. He may have saved her from her own hair-brained scheme, but he'd been more than repaid for that kindness already. "Lord Suffolk will not be pleased when he learns of this, the two are bitter enemies, father."

He shrugged. "I don't plan to tell him. Do you?"

Well, no, she didn't. It would lead to more jealousy, and more demands for physical placation. She shook her head.

"I thought as much." Hereford stood and gestured to Julia and Margaret to do the same. "Be on your best behavior, daughter. Don't embarrass me any further than you already have."

Julia followed her father into the hallway with a sigh. The man was a selfish drunkard, yet he always managed to make her feel like a ninny. In fact, once Sebastian met the Viscount he would likely lose all interest. Only a bedlamite, or a blackguard in desperate straits like Thomas Howard, would want Henry Deveraux as an acquaintance. That would solve her problem once and for all. It was what she wanted, wasn't it?

No, her heart screamed, as she entered the parlor and caught sight of him. Sebastian was dressed to the nines, with black hessians, tan breeches, tan waistcoat, and a dark brown overcoat. His cravat, tied in an elaborate pattern, was secured with a pin that held a single, brilliant ruby in its center, surrounded by a circle of diamonds. Julia's eyes were also drawn to a ring on his right hand, again made of rubies and diamonds in a gold setting. His watch fob was intricately engraved with what she assumed to be the Rutland seal. He'd never worn jewelry before that she had noticed. Was he trying to impress her father? The old man was fairly drooling; whatever Sebastian's plan, it was working.

"Your grace, what a pleasure," Hereford began, stepping forward with a bow.

"Viscount, the pleasure is mine," Sebastian returned the bow, before turning to the women. "Lady Margaret, Miss Deveraux."

"Good morning, your Grace," Julia inclined her head.

Aunt Margaret curtsied, and looked about to faint again.

"I assume Miss Deveraux told you that she befell some misfortune and took a nasty blow to the head near my estate, which is how she found herself in my care."

Henry nodded. "Yes, your Grace, and I am very grateful for

your assistance in the matter. If I had known where she was, I would have sent for her post haste, rather than burden you with her upkeep."

Sebastian waved a gloved hand. "It was no burden, my lord. I so rarely have visitors at Foxwaith, it was refreshing. I dare say she has inspired me to venture back into London again, after a prolonged absence."

"I have no business asking, Lord Rutland," Henry said, "but I would appreciate your discretion in regards to Julia's whereabouts. I managed to keep the rumors at bay by saying she was in the country, recovering from an illness."

"You'll hear no contradictions from me. That is, in fact, partially true. I see no reason to disclose details of where and why to anyone."

"It would benefit your own reputation as well, I'm sure you realize," Margaret finally spoke up. She looked thoroughly smitten. Heavens, the man had the ability to charm anyone.

"You may have noticed, my lady, that I haven't much of a reputation anyway," he replied.

"You no doubt put those nasty rumors about your person to bed last night, by appearing at the Tilsdale's ball, your Grace. Everyone quite plainly saw they were untrue."

Anders appeared with a tray of tea and biscuits. In his usual, unobtrusive way, he deposited them onto the table and left again. Julia busied herself by pouring tea for everyone. When she handed Sebastian his cup, his fingers brushed against hers, the lightest of touches.

"I have two reasons for my visit today, Lord Hereford," Sebastian said, taking a seat.

"Oh yes, I, ah …" Her father fumbled with his watch fob. "I realize you are out some coin on my daughter's behalf. If you will tell me the amount, I'll be sure to gather it in the next day or two."

She resisted the urge to snort. Her father was destitute and everyone, including Sebastian, knew it.

"That's not why I came." There was another dismissive

wave of his hand. It was strange seeing him act so ducal. "I've returned your stallion."

"Oh?" The old man fairly swooned for joy.

"I had my horse master look him over before we left Lincolnshire, and he is in perfect health. I also had him shod for you."

"You did?" Henry's voice had risen an octave.

Julia's eyes narrowed. What was Sebastian playing at? First Thomas satisfies her father's debts at White's, and now Sebastian pays for the upkeep of that silly horse? Was he trying to purchase her affections? Or bribe her back into his bed?

What if he did it because he truly cares for you? That stupid inner voice was back. She tried to push it away.

"It's a magnificent animal," Sebastian was saying, drawing her back to attention, "I can't imagine you were pleased to part with it."

"I … your Grace, I don't know what to say. You are very generous."

"Think nothing of it. I would like to inquire, however, if Miss Deveraux is free today."

"No," Julia said, at the same moment her father replied, "yes."

"I brought my phaeton; I thought perhaps we could go for a ride to Hyde Park. With you as chaperon of course, Lady Margaret."

"No!" Julia said again.

"Yes!" Aunt Margaret exclaimed.

Sebastian regarded them with an amused smile.

"I've no objections, your Grace," Henry said.

"Perhaps you'd like to take your stallion out for a ride, now that he's been returned, Lord Hereford?" Sebastian suggested.

"Ah, oh, um, yes. What a splendid idea."

"Then it's settled." He offered his arm to Julia. She had no choice but to take it. "Shall we?"

•

Sebastian learned two things very quickly. First, Julia would rather be anywhere than with him. She made certain to look at everything but him. And second, her aunt Margaret couldn't hear a thing. At first he'd thought the woman rude for ignoring his attempts at inane conversation. Then he realized that she was simply deaf. The first revelation was discouraging; the second could work in his favor. He'd been trying to find a way to get Julia alone, and here in London with all its damn society dictates, that was nigh impossible. Since her chaperone was oblivious to anything he said so long as he spoke in relatively subdued tones, it didn't matter if she were present or not. Before they'd even reached the park, the old woman was sound asleep anyway.

It was a particularly nice day for London, bright and sunny with a mild breeze, and either he had finally acclimated to the stench, or it was less permeating in the park, because for the first time since he'd arrived in Town, his olfactory senses weren't on overload. He welcomed the change. The park was predictably congested, filled with men and women engaged in the equally predictable task of pursuing affections. It was an activity which Sebastian himself was also intent upon exploring.

He knew he faced a challenge. Julia gave no indication she would bend her resolve any time soon. Still, he had to try. It was his solitary purpose of late.

"I think your father likes me," Sebastian said, trying to find a way to begin the conversation. He winced. Not the smoothest opening line.

Julia laughed, but it didn't reach her eyes. "Throw your money at him, and my father will agree to anything. I thought you knew that."

Damn. "He had every right to call me out, actually."

"Do you honestly think I'm stupid enough to tell him what we did?"

"No. That's not what I meant."

Her lips were drawn into a thin line. "I'm not pleased that you are bribing my father with your coffers, Sebastian. It's exactly what Thomas is doing."

He took a deep breath. Then another, and another, until the urge to steer the phaeton into a tree had passed. "I thought to do something nice for you, and your father. It wasn't a bribe."

"Well it seemed like one."

"Well it wasn't."

"Fine." Julia folded her hands in her lap and scowled at a passing tree. If looks could kill, the poor thing would have withered on the spot.

"Fine!"

"You're acting like a child."

"I am not," he countered. She arched an eyebrow but kept silent. "Woman, you make me crazy." She did, too. He'd spent well over an hour debating his cravat pin this morning. He hadn't even bothered with the damn things for years, but Catherine had thought it a nice touch, along with the ring Queen Anne had given his ancestor, the first Duke of Rutland. And when his sister suggested he also select a cane, he'd expected his head to explode.

"Then perhaps you should not call on me again. I wouldn't want to be the reason you find yourself in Bedlam, your Grace."

"It's worse without you." He had to soften her resolve, but how? "I wish you'd let me explain what you overheard that day. It's not what you think."

Her hands fidgeted with the folds of her gown. "You were very clear, actually," she replied. "Besides, every time I allow you to explain yourself I end up in a compromising position."

That was true. He wouldn't mind another chance to get her in his bed, though. "We're in the middle of Hyde Park in broad daylight, sweetheart," he answered instead. "There's little danger of anything happening here."

"Humph."

He sighed and steered the carriage past a pair of slow-moving grays. "It pains me to see you so angry with me."

"I'm not angry. I'm hurt."

On second thought, anger would be better. He couldn't live with himself knowing he'd broken her heart. His own memories of heartbreak were difficult enough to bear. "That pains me, too. What can I do to change your opinion of me?"

Finally, she looked at him. "Nothing."

"Suppose I kidnap you and whisk you away?"

"My god, do you think you're a hero in one of Mrs. Radcliffe's novels?" Julia asked.

"If I have to be, to win you back," he replied. Wouldn't Catherine be pleased by such a romantic strategy? "How about I court you?"

"What?"

Her shout was loud enough to wake Lady Margaret, who sat upright with a start. "What did you say, dear?"

"I told Miss Deveraux that I would like to court her, Lady Margaret," Sebastian supplied, making sure his voice was loud enough for the old woman to hear. Julia's expression alternated from shock to fury and back again.

"Yes, Aunt, and I told him that I am already engaged."

Margaret regarded them both through narrowed eyes. "Not officially, you aren't."

"Exactly," Julia continued, "so there is absolutely no way I could possibly— What?"

"Has he proposed to you, or only spoken to my brother on the matter?"

"Well, just Father—"

"And has he given you a ring?"

"No."

"Have the banns been posted? Has Lord Suffolk made any announcement to his friends? Or you to yours for that matter?"

Julia's brow furrowed. "Well, no."

"Then you aren't engaged."

These were mere technicalities. Surely the old woman knew that, even if she'd never married herself. At that moment, Margaret caught his eye over Julia's lap and winked. Sebastian couldn't prevent a grin. Did he actually have an ally in Julia's aunt? His wounded heart leapt. Perhaps he had a chance, after all.

•

"So, did you have a nice day?" Henry asked that night at dinner. He was three sheets to the wind already, and had been since mid-afternoon. Julia suspected the only reason he was present at the table and not already at the club was curiosity.

"I suppose," she replied, pushing a cube of beef around her plate.

"What did his Grace speak to you about?"

She sighed. "Nothing."

"Oh, that's hardly true, dear," Aunt Margaret spoke up, spearing a carrot slice with her fork. "He asked to court her, Henry."

Her father's eyes lit up. "Did he?"

"Yes," she admitted sourly. "But I told him it was out of the question."

"Why in the hell would you do that?"

She set her fork down and glared at him. "Have you forgotten I'm already engaged to the Earl?"

Henry rolled his eyes. "What does that have to do with anything? If I have the choice between a duke and an earl for a son-in-law, I choose a duke."

"Well, you don't have a choice, Father."

"He's quite smitten, Henry," Margaret supplied with glee.

"Julia, I advise you to encourage his Grace's suit."

"And why would that be? Because he's rolling in money, perhaps?"

Henry grinned. "I see nothing wrong with wanting my daughter to live in comfort, and to marry well."

"Lord Thomas has already spent money on your behalf to satisfy your debts at White's. I can't back out of our arrangement now."

"I don't see why not. Rutland can pay the man off, can't he?"

Julia stood and dropped her napkin to the table. "Suppose he chooses not to? Suppose he is of the same mind as Grandfather was when it comes to being your source of income?"

"I suspect you can persuade him whichever way you choose. You were so angry with me when I struck the deal with Suffolk that you ran away. Now, you have a chance to avoid the entire affair. I don't see why you won't take it."

"Yes, that's precisely the problem. You never see, do you, Father?" Turning on her heel she stalked from the room, and went directly to her bedchamber, locking the door behind her. Struggling out of her clothes, she dropped a simple cotton nightgown over her head and took a seat at her vanity with a sigh. She removed the pins from her hair and began to brush out the long black locks using steady strokes.

She'd returned home to discover most of the staff absent; those who hadn't quit for lack of payment had been fired by her father, and her abigail, Lizzie, had been amongst the casualties. The Viscount, after learning of Julia's absence, had correctly deduced Lizzie's involvement in the scheme, and dismissed her along with anyone who helped carry it out.

Only the cook and her young daughter, Henry's valet, the stable hand, and the ever-faithful Anders remained. Julia could manage just fine on her own, but Lizzie had been her faithful companion for years. Now, she had no one to talk to at all.

And she needed someone to talk to. More now than ever before. Fate was either very cruel or very bored, or both. A week ago, her strongest desire was to have Sebastian formally courting her, her father's approval of the match, and an escape from Thomas Howard. Of the two choices, was Thomas really the better one? Why was Sebastian so skilled at building hope within her only to crush it under his boot heel?

Again, she felt it swelling, that glimmer of anticipation that perhaps she might live happily after all. This time, she was fighting it as hard as she could, but he was relentless and now backed by her father and her aunt. He'd asked for another chance. She didn't want to say yes, but she did not have the resolve to say no.

Was it revenge that fueled Sebastian's pursuit, or was it love?

Love, her heart whispered with interminable optimism. *He came to London, for you. It must be love.*

Through the film of tears in her eyes, Julia smiled.

Chapter Thirteen

Sebastian surveyed the crowded theater with a frustrated sigh. Where was she? Lady Margaret and Julia had agreed to his invitation tonight, and he'd gained use of Alex's box for the occasion. Both of his siblings had wanted to come tonight also, but he'd instructed them to seek amusement elsewhere, under pain of death. The performance would be starting soon, and his guests had yet to arrive.

He had been stalking various society functions in the hopes of encountering Julia, and on the whole, he'd been highly successful. Margaret had definitely proven herself to be his ally over the last week. At the Marbury's soirée she'd dragged Julia over to a row of chairs along the wall feigning fatigue when he had been standing conveniently nearby, giving him the opportunity to request a dance. When Lord Hayburn had claimed the seat next to Julia at the Reardon's dinner party the following night, Margaret accidentally tipped the gravy boat into the man's lap, and when he left the table to clean up, Sebastian took his place. Suffolk, seated across the table next to Lady Marbury, had slammed his wine down with a scowl, but wisely kept his mouth shut.

Sebastian also suspected that Margaret's hearing was not impaired, after all. Her deafness came and went in selective situations, such as when seated next to the longwinded Lord Martin, who thought everyone was as interested in his family history as he, or when the trio went riding in the park.

He wasn't keeping score, of course, that would be childish.

But when one compared the twenty-two dances he'd shared with Julia in the last week to the fourteen she'd granted Suffolk, it became clear things were looking up. She hadn't called him a bedlamite in three days, and she'd stopped saying "I hate you" after dance sixteen. During dance eighteen he noticed she was wearing rosewater perfume again. Last night upon seeing him at Almack's, she actually smiled. Yes, he was making progress. He suspected Julia's continued resistance was more a result of her infernal stubbornness than lingering anger.

"... don't think they were properly cooked," Lady Margaret's voice drifted in from the hallway, bringing him out of his thoughts. A moment later she entered the box, with Julia in tow. "Ah, your Grace, good evening. I was just mentioning the lobster patties from last night, they were most disagreeable, didn't you think?"

Sebastian stood and kissed her gloved hand in greeting. "I confess I paid no attention to the refreshments. You are not ill, I trust?"

"Oh no, thank goodness, but I won't be having those again any time soon you can be sure. They gave me fits." She picked her way to the front of the box and took the leftmost seat. "No, we were late because my niece here redid her hair three times and changed her dress twice. Then there was a terrible congestion outside, I was worried we would miss the opening curtain."

He turned to Julia, who was blushing an endearing shade of pink. "Your niece looks beautiful, as always. I am quite certain it's not the dress' doing. But you are here and so all is well."

"I didn't. I mean, I wasn't," Julia sputtered, turning from pink to red.

"It's not her fault," Margaret continued, snapping open her fan. "Personally, I don't mind the lack of servants; being a woman past her prime has its advantages in that I don't much care how my hair looks, but for a young girl on the marriage mart, it's quite awful."

"Where did the servants go?"

Margaret rolled her eyes. "Those that didn't quit, Henry ran off."

"I see." He didn't, really, but given Julia's mortified expression, he didn't press the issue. "I believe the curtain is about to rise, ladies. This version of *Taming of the Shrew* is supposed to be quite captivating." And, somehow, fitting.

Julia went to sit next to her aunt, who immediately dropped her reticule on the seat to her right, leaving only one other chair in the front row open—the one next to Sebastian. She eyed him hesitantly, then nodded.

You are a saint, Lady Margaret, he praised silently.

As the play began, Sebastian tried his best to pay attention to the actors on stage instead of the woman beside him, for the first few minutes at least. Before long, he simply gave up. His gaze traced the smooth line of her nose, the delicate curve of her neck, and the generous swell of her breasts. Her profile was perfect, and with the soft illumination from the stage creating a glowing outline, she looked ethereal, like an angel.

She must have sensed he was staring, because she turned and met his gaze. "What?" she whispered.

"You are so …" He searched for the right word. "Perfect."

"Don't be ridiculous. I am not."

He couldn't help himself. Stretching out a hand he traced his fingers along the bare skin of her arm. "Yes, you are."

"Sebastian, no!"

His fingers had drifted, stroking her side, her hip, really anywhere he could touch without drawing attention. "No one can see, sweetheart."

"Aunt Margaret …"

"Is sound asleep." Or at least pretending to be; she'd had her head cocked back, eyes shut, and her mouth open since Lucentio realized his love for Bianca in the first scene. Either option suited him just fine, and her presence, limited though it was, did force him to employ more restraint than he would have if they'd been alone.

"She could wake up, you know," Julia murmured. Her touch

was light and cool against his arm, but instead of pushing him away, she laced their fingers together and drew his hand into her lap.

He could have cried. Bloody hell, he was going to cry if he wasn't careful. By her own initiation and free will, she'd touched him. She was still touching him! Now he really was acting like a bedlamite. He'd learned to maintain an iron grip on his control, and to appreciate the small victories with Julia, but his patience was dwindling with each passing moment. It was time for a new tactic. Thanks to Alex's overly detailed stories of the theater, he had a plan.

They were still holding hands at the end of the third act, when intermission was called. It was only at Lady Margaret's stirring that Julia pulled her hand away. Sebastian stood, relieved at the opportunity to stretch his aching legs.

"My dear ladies," he said, "would you care to take a turn with me around the lobby, or perhaps the gardens? I am in need of fresh air." He was in need of ten minutes alone with Julia, in a darkened garden.

"Climb down those awful stairs only to come back up and then have to descend a second time?" Margaret scoffed. "No thank you."

Julia looked disappointed for a moment, then she nodded. "We will stay, Lord Rutland."

"No," Margaret replied, "I will stay. You two will go."

"I suppose I could use a stretch."

"Of course you could, dear. Now go with his Grace."

He really would have to thank Lady Margaret somehow for her help. A rather large gift of some kind would do it. Perhaps she'd like to come live at Foxwaith niece once he and Julia were married. He got the sense she cared not for London, or Viscount Hereford, any more than he did. She could be close to her niece and grand nephew, who Sebastian hoped to see arriving in short order.

Julia placed her hand on his offered arm, and strolled with him out of the box, down the stairs, and into the lobby. The space was crowded with patrons, all of them milling about, engaging in idle conversation as they waited for the play to resume. He steered them toward the back door, which led to a large, covered balcony and the small gardens beyond.

"Where are we going?" Julia asked.

"To the gardens. It's much too stuffy in here with all these people."

"We could end up alone out there," she said.

God, I hope so. That was, after all, the plan.

•

"You'll be safe with me, Miss Deveraux."

She smiled. "Of course I will be, that's not the point." In truth, she was looking forward to time alone with Sebastian, but she had to keep her head. They were at the theater, and it seemed the entire ton was with them, watching them.

He guided her onto the balcony, and down the steps into the garden. Once they were several paces out of the light cast from the open doors of the lobby, he detached her hand from his arm, and laced their fingers together. Even through the cloth of their gloves, she could feel the warmth and strength of his skin.

He started to pull her off the path and into a small copse of bushes. "Your Grace, I do not think this wise!"

"Oh? Why not?"

"The first thing a young woman learns upon emergence into society is to never, ever, under any circumstances venture alone with a man into the bushes," she stated, but when he gave her hand a gentle tug her feet moved of their own accord, away from the balcony and deeper into the shadows of the garden.

"Well then, I'd say you're being a very naughty debutante, my dear."

"Sebastian, please take me back before—mmph!" His mouth covered hers and stifled of her protestations. He really shouldn't be kissing her here, if they were discovered, it would be scandal for them both.

But she couldn't think of a single thing she wanted to be doing more than this. It was as wonderful as she remembered, and with her eyes closed, in his arms this way, she could almost pretend they were back at Fowaith. His scent, his taste, made her feel safe—and loved.

A woman laughed in the distance, and it startled Julia out of her reverie. "Sebastian, stop," she said, breaking the kiss. It was a weak protest, a fact upon which he commented without delay.

"Do you really want me to?" His breath was a warm against her cheek.

"No. I mean yes!" His lips closed around her earlobe and she sighed. "My logical side is telling me to kick you and run away." It would be the only way she could summon the willpower to leave his side. So long as his lips were on her skin, she was staying right here.

"Is it?" Strong fingers were stroking her arms and shoulders, undeterred. "And do you have an illogical side?"

"Yes." Heavens, did she ever.

"What is it telling you?"

She twined her arms around his neck. "That we need to find a better hiding spot."

"Ah. Since I don't fancy being kicked, even by someone as lovely as you, I must agree with your illogical side. That makes the vote two against one."

"Don't you have a logical side?" she asked.

"Not around you I don't."

"But if we're discovered—"

"Then you'll have to marry me, sweetheart. I can think of worse fates, can't you?"

Why yes, she could. That wasn't the point. "Oh, to hell with the point!"

"I beg your pardon?"

One of these days, she was going to learn to separate her internal and external monologues. Strange that it only happened around him. "Just kiss me again."

He did. Julia melted against him, hands clutching the lapels of his jacket, and when her knees buckled his arms were there, holding her against him. It was just where she was meant to be. Now she understood why kissing Thomas was so different; she wasn't in love with him. The missing ingredient had been love. After a long moment, he broke the kiss, and she whimpered.

"We need to go back," Sebastian said.

"Why?"

He sighed and brushed a lock of hair from her forehead. Her coiffeur was likely hopeless. "For one thing, we're missing Act Four."

"I don't care about the play, Sebastian," she replied.

"No, neither do I, but for appearance sake, we have to play the society game."

He was right. "Okay, let's go."

"No, we need to return separately. You go first; head for the ladies retiring room and fix your, um...dress." His voice sounded strained. "Wait five minutes, then go back to the box, I'll be there."

She nodded and kissed his cheek, then made her way back to the balcony and back into the theater lobby. It was empty save a few attendants and footmen, the patrons having returned to their seats for the second half of the performance. The retiring room was to the right of the lobby, down a hall that led to the auditorium's side entrances, and she hurried through the door as quickly as possible without drawing attention to herself. Thank goodness the play had already resumed, she was a mess.

Checking the clock on the mantle, she set to work attempting to fix her hair, which was difficult without a brush. The small mirror propped next to the clock revealed a disheveled woman with flushed cheeks and swollen lips. In short, she looked as if she'd been kissed quite thoroughly, which of course she had.

He'd mentioned marriage again. She didn't want him to be forced to the altar amidst rumor and scandal, but if he proposed, she would accept.

The door creaked open behind her and she prayed silently that it would not be Lady Marbury or worse, Lady Maxcomb. The deep baritone indicated her visitor was, in fact, someone much worse.

"Did you enjoy your little expedition into the foliage, love?"

"Pardon?" She turned to face the intruder.

Thomas snorted. One hand on his hip, the other gripping his cane, he regarded her with a wry smirk. "I saw you disappear into the bushes with Rutland."

Julia fought the urge to curse aloud. She'd expanded her vocabulary of late, thanks to her recent male acquaintances, and had confidence she could do so quite capably. "His grace accompanied me on a stroll around the gardens, my lord, that's all."

"That would be a plausible story, were your hair not helplessly mussed and your clothing rumpled."

"I fell."

"Of course you did, angel." He took a step forward, then another. She resisted the urge to back away from him, and stood her ground. He couldn't bully her, not anymore. "I've warned your suitor numerous times to stay away from you. It's clear he hasn't been listening. This time, I'm warning you."

"Warning me of what?" She didn't understand why his smile made her nauseous, while Sebastian's made her feel safe.

"Stay away from him, Julia. You're mine."

"Am I?"

He grabbed her by the arms. "Yes, you are. I can and will ruin you both if you try to cross me."

"If …" She paused, took a deep breath. She could do this. "If you tell anyone where I was these last few weeks, all it will do is force Sebastian and I to marry. Isn't that the opposite of what you want?"

Thomas scowled and shook her. "Revealing your whereabouts will ruin you. Revealing his engagement to

Amelia Cartwright is what will ruin him."

"That would be your word against his and nothing more."

"Are you certain? I wouldn't be, if I were you," he warned. His tone was dark, menacing. She believed he was telling the truth.

"I'll speak to him," Julia said.

"See that you do, love. If you won't remove him from the equation, I'll do it myself. Permanently, if I must. You know…" Taking her face between his palms he bent down until their lips were nearly touching. "There are worse things I can do than spread rumors."

•

He was about to go looking for her when the door to the box slid open and Julia stepped inside. She'd been gone twice as long as he'd instructed, and looked no less disheveled now than before. What happened? It was hard to make out her facial expression in the dimly lit ambiance, so he couldn't tell if she was upset or not.

"Are you alright, sweetheart?" he whispered as she took her seat, casting a glance at the slumbering Lady Margaret.

"Yes," she replied. "I was speaking with Lady Amanda in the retiring room is all."

"Are you certain?" Her posture was stiff, and there was something off in her voice. He sensed something had distressed her.

"I'm fine, Sebastian. But I think perhaps Aunt Margaret and I should leave before the play ends."

She wasn't fine, he could tell. "Are you sure you're alright? Have you taken ill?"

"I'm alright. My hair is not." Julia gestured to the tangled mass of curls at her nape. "Best to leave before the rest of the ton have the chance to see me. Tongues will wag."

That was true. "Alright, I'll see you home now, if you'd like."

"Our carriage didn't wait for us, he was to return in a few hours."

"We'll take mine."

They roused Lady Margaret and made their way outside, where Sebastian's coachman was waiting. A few minutes of waiting while he retrieved the carriage, and they were safely on their way. Julia was silent, and Margaret miraculously managed to stay awake for once.

"May I call on you tomorrow?" he asked as they approached the Viscount's townhome.

For a moment she looked like she was going to say 'no.' "Yes, I'd like that."

"Good. I was thinking we could stroll Bond Street, maybe take a ride in the park."

"Okay." She smiled. "Tomorrow then."

The ride back to Rutland House was, thankfully, short. He had plans to set in motion.

His siblings were waiting for him in the study.

"Well," Catherine said, "how did it go?"

Sebastian shook his head. "Why are you here so late?"

"Waiting for you, of course. We want details." Alex handed him a tumbler. "Juicy ones if possible."

"The play was tolerable. Lady Margaret disliked the lobster patties at Almack's last night, but she had recovered by morning."

Alex's nose wrinkled in disgust. "That's not the sort of details I am after, and you know it. Did you make use of the bushes? Any trouble finding my spot?"

"Your spot? Alexander!" Catherine exclaimed. "Don't tell me you're luring women into the bushes. And you better not have followed his example, Sebastian!"

He took a swill of his drink and chuckled. He hadn't planned on sharing, but it would be fun to horrify his sister a bit. "We found our own spot, actually. Wouldn't want to soil yours with memories of me, and vice versa."

"Sebastian, honestly!"

"Yes, Sebastian," Alex repeated, "honestly. That spot works just fine, and it wouldn't be your memory I'd reminisce about, it would be the lady's."

"Alex, don't," Sebastian growled. "Not tonight. I have things to do."

"Things? What things? Marriage related things?"

"As a matter of fact, dear sister, yes." Julia had given him the confidence he needed.

Alex slapped his thigh and whooped. "Hallelujah!"

"Don't get your hopes up yet. I'm going to propose tomorrow. I need to speak with the solicitor, and I'd like to purchase a ring."

"What about Mother's ring? The one Father gave her?" Catherine suggested.

"It's at Foxwaith."

His sister smiled. "No it's not."

"You brought it with us?"

"Naturally. You were coming to London to win her back. I thought it might come in handy."

Chapter Fourteen

*T*he night was dreary and damp to match her mood. A blanket of fog clung to her ankles as she made her way from the carriage to the door of Thomas' London townhome. She'd snuck out after Aunt Margaret retired to her room and the servants went to bed. Henry was at the club, where he went every night of late, returning at breakfast, completely foxed. No one saw her leave. She walked to the end of the street and managed, against all odds, to find a hackney. The driver didn't hide the fact he thought her to be a lightskirt and she didn't bother to correct him. After all, what honest well-bred lady would be traveling alone at night in a hired carriage? It was most definitely bad ton.

She didn't have a choice.

The man who opened the door was elderly, with graying hair and a slightly stooped posture. "Yes?" he asked.

"I must speak with Lord Suffolk."

"He is not here." His tone was haughty.

She lifted her chin. "Then I will wait."

"Madam, his lordship does not like people to be here without him, particularly not women of your status."

"Of my status?" That was it. "I am no whore. I am Miss Deveraux, the earl's fiancée."

The butler blanched, and made a strangled noise in his throat. "I... um... my lady." He bowed. "Please accept my profound apologies. I only assumed — Does his lordship expect you?"

"No, I doubt it. But it's important that I speak with him tonight. May I come in and wait?"

"Yes, my lady, of course." He ushered her inside and took her cloak, then showed her to Thomas' study. "I'll get you some tea. Perhaps you'd like some cakes?"

"That would be lovely. Thank you, Mr—"

He bowed again. "My name is Edwards. I'm his lordship's butler."

"Nice to meet you, Edwards."

At the door he stopped and turned. "My lady? I— Are you going to tell Lord Suffolk how I insulted you tonight?"

"I don't see any reason to," she replied.

Some of his color was finally returning. Were the servants as afraid of Thomas as the ton? It seemed so. "Thank you, my lady. Thank you."

The door clicked shut and she let out a relieved sigh. She understood being afraid of Thomas. Fear had motivated her own clandestine visit to his townhome. She believed his threat. Her goal was to convince him to leave Sebastian alone. Tomorrow, when Sebastian came to call, she'd convince him to return to Foxwaith. Then, she'd marry Thomas. She didn't have a choice.

For now she had to ensure Thomas knew of her commitment, by whatever means necessary. If he demanded she spend the night to prove it, then she would do so. To save Sebastian's life, she would.

The butler returned with a tray of tea and cakes. He bowed and left, shutting the door behind him. Julia surveyed her surroundings; a large oak desk sat at the far end of the room. Shelves lined each wall save one, which held a large fireplace. Why had Edwards put her here rather than the parlor? It was strange. Most men were odd about their studies; Sebastian kept the door to his locked when he wasn't in it, and she'd never seen the inside of her father's at all. Studies were where gentlemen hid their important papers …

The proof Thomas claimed to have of Sebastian's engagement

to Lady Amelia—was it here? If she could find it, perhaps she would gain the advantage.

Alright, where would it be? She stood in the center of the room, hands on her hips, and turned in a slow circle. Behind the books? Maybe. A secret cubby behind the fireplace mantle? She'd been reading too many novels. The most logical place to start was the desk. The top drawer contained stacks of bank notes, and small pouches she assumed to be filled with coin.

The middle drawer had correspondence, mostly from Thomas' solicitor and business associates. It seemed her fiancé owned interests in several shipping companies which dealt with trade with America, and a number of establishments in east London that she suspected were less than reputable gentleman's clubs. *Interesting*.

The bottom drawer contained accounting ledgers, dozens of them, stacked neatly in columns. All were handbound in dark blue leather ... save one. At the bottom of the leftmost stack was a different type of book, slightly larger than the rest and made with dark red leather. Lifting out the books she pulled it free. The top corner was engraved with the letters AC.

Amelia Cartwright?

She flipped open the cover. It was a journal, written in a delicate, female hand. My god, was it really hers?

Each entry was dated, with the last being five years ago, almost to the day. Julia picked one toward the end and started to read. It was Amelia's, it had to be.

> *I have met a wonderful gentleman. Father is skeptical, but Mother is thrilled. She's always wanted me to be a duchess, and Sebastian will be a duke. He is kind, considerate, and generous, showering me with gifts and trinkets.*

Julia skipped forward.

> *I have never felt so torn. Sebastian is the perfect gentleman, and I know he would be a fine husband, but last week at*

Almack's I met Lord Thomas, son of the Earl of Suffolk. He is everything Sebastian is not – dark, dangerous, and far more forward than he should be. For some reason, I cannot stop thinking about him. Father and Mother do not approve. Thomas says I must follow my heart. I have not told Sebastian of Thomas' attentions, or my feelings.

June 3. Sebastian has asked for my hand, and I have accepted. I know I must tell him about Thomas before we wed, and I fear that when he learns what I have done, he will never want to speak to me again. I cannot blame him. I betrayed his trust…

June 12. Sebastian knows. He discovered Thomas and I tonight. I saw the hurt in his eyes, the shame. It is for the best if he breaks our engagement now. I am with child. Thomas's child. There is no way I can marry Sebastian now. Thomas will offer for me when he learns of the baby; he has to. If he loves me as he claims, we will be married and live happily. Mother said once that everything happens for a reason. I must believe that now.

June 13. Thomas laughed when I told him about the child. He laughed! He said he would enjoy watching Sebastian raise his bastard, and knowing that a Howard would be the next Duke of Rutland. But Sebastian will never speak to me again, and even if he changes his mind, I will not marry him. I am going to speak with Thomas one last time tonight. If he again refuses to see reason, then I will go to my father. Father will force a marriage between us. It will not be the happy arrangement I had hoped for, at least not at first, but my child will not be born a bastard. Thomas must finish what he has started.

Julia shut the book and pressed a hand to her mouth. Amelia's final entry was not written by a woman about to take her own life. But if it hadn't been suicide, then it had been murder. She had a good idea who.

This was Thomas' so-called proof? Why would he keep something so incriminating? Well, whatever the reason, she was grateful for it. It could be the proof she needed to save Sebastian.

Sebastian! She had to show him what she'd found. All the time he'd spent blaming himself for Amelia's death, and it had never been his fault. She would show him the journal and tell him everything. Together, they would decide what to do.

"Are you alright, my lady?" Edwards poked his head in the door.

"I'm fine, but I've changed my mind. I don't want to wait for his lordship after all."

"Of course, my lady. I'll retrieve your cloak."

"Edwards?" she asked. "Please, don't tell him I was here tonight."

"I won't. You have my word."

•

It was bloody late. The clock chimed midnight just as Sebastian's solicitor, Mr. Johnson, was putting the last stack of paper into his bag. Everything was in order for tomorrow. All he required now was courage.

He showed Mr. Johnson out, and was just ascending the stairs toward his bedchamber when the doorbell chimed. What had the man forgotten? With a sigh, Sebastian turned and headed back down the stairs again. The staff had been sent to bed hours ago, so he'd answer the door himself.

"Mr. Johnson, I don't believe you—" It wasn't his elderly, overweight solicitor in the doorway, but a woman. Silky black hair spilled from beneath the hood of her cape. He knew that hair. "Julia?"

"Sebastian." She lifted her head, and drew back the hood.

"What the bloody hell are you doing here?"

"I came to speak to you. May I come in?"

He stepped back and let her step inside. "How did you get

here?"

"Hackney," she replied, shaking the rain from her cape, and pulling off her gloves.

He coughed and stared at her. "You took a hack?"

"Yes. Sebastian, I need to tell you something."

"Woman, have you gone mad? It's past midnight!" Sebastian rubbed his forehead, trying to chase off the headache that was forming. This was insanity.

She laid a hand on his arm. "Where can we talk?"

"How about in my carriage while I take you home? Your father is going to have fits when he finds you gone." He started to pace. How could he deliver her safely home and back upstairs without Henry discovering them?

"My father is off somewhere three sheets to the wind as usual. Sebastian, it's Thomas."

That stopped him. "What about Thomas?"

"It wasn't Lady Amanda who spoke to me tonight in the retiring room, it was Thomas."

"What?" A door creaked open upstairs. With a sigh he ushered her into the parlor and shut the door before his brother—who was actually home and in bed for once—came to investigate.

"He saw us go into the garden. He threatened me, or I suppose to be accurate, he threatened you."

The bastard. "What did he say? Did he harm you?"

"No, he just frightened me." Julia slipped her cloak from her shoulders and set it on the sofa. "He said that he had proof of your involvement with Amelia five years ago. That if I didn't stop seeing you and marry him, he would show everyone in the ton. And if that didn't work, that he would kill you."

A muscle in his jaw ticked. "Not if I kill him first."

"That's why I went to his house tonight."

"You did what?" Oh bloody hell, he was shouting again.

"I went to his house to reason with him," she repeated calmly. "He wasn't there. So I searched his study. I found …" She held up a leather bound book or ledger of some sort. "I found this. Sebastian, you need to read it."

He took it from her hands and turned it over. The letters AC were engraved in the top corner, and he ran a shaking finger over them. AC ... Amelia? Flipping through the pages, he saw his name.

"I have met a wonderful gentleman. Father is skeptical, but Mother is thrilled. She's always wanted me to be a duchess, and Sebastian will be a duke ..." His head snapped up. Julia had perched on the edge of the sofa beside her cloak and was watching him, hands folded in her lap. He returned to the diary and began to pace again as he read. By the time he reached the June twelfth entry, he felt lightheaded. Would Julia think less of him if he suffered an attack of the vapors? Because one was not far off.

His mind was reeling. *She never loved me.* Hell, that wasn't even the worst of it.

"Sebastian," Julia interrupted. Her voice was gentle. "Do you remember what day Amelia died?"

"June fourteenth," he replied. The day after her final entry. According to this, she had gone to see Thomas the night before her body was found.

"I don't think she killed herself."

His next thought exactly. "Then that would mean—"

"That would mean she was murdered," Julia supplied. "And whoever murdered her, made it look like a suicide. There's only one person I can think of who had reason to want her dead."

He hated Thomas Howard, but did he think the man capable of murder? "This isn't proof," he said.

"It's proof of one thing."

"What?"

Julia stood and crossed the room to him. Laying a palm against his cheek she whispered, "You were never to blame."

That couldn't be true. He had five years of pain and guilt weighing on his heart. He was guilty of something, surely. "I could have forgiven her. Married her. Protected her."

"No, Sebastian," she shook her head. "She didn't want you to."

"I thought she loved me." For some reason, it hardly seemed to matter now.

"I know, and I'm sorry. But I love you, Sebastian." She searched his face. Her expression was pleading, her eyes fresh with unshed tears. "You're infuriating and pig-headed and — and I love you. Don't you see? You're free now. No more guilt or shame."

No more guilt? He'd lived with it for so long, could he really let go? With her, his heart whispered, you can. "I love you, too," he said finally. His own tears pricked at his eyelids; he blinked them away. "Julia, I love you."

She smiled. "After everything you've put me through, Sebastian Cade, you'd better."

Well. He hadn't expected that for a reaction. Still, it could have been worse. "I should get you home."

"You could. Or you could get me upstairs."

His laugh was genuine. Minx. She knew he couldn't turn down a request such as that. Engaged was a good as married, wasn't it? The portion of his anatomy currently crowding his breeches insisted it was. "Sweetheart, that's the second time you've asked me to take you to my bedroom."

"Yes, and?"

"I didn't say 'no,' then," he replied, lifting her into his arms. "And I don't plan to say 'no' now."

Alex's door creaked open as they passed. His brother's head appeared, hair mussed, eyes squinting. "What is that noi— Oh bloody hell," he muttered upon seeing Julia. The door clicked shut again. "Carry on!"

Sebastian expected her to be mortified. Instead, she giggled. "No need to worry about waking him," she said, "since we've already done so. Though perhaps we should have a care to be quiet."

"Put all thoughts of my brother from your mind, sweetheart."

One eyebrow lifted. "Make me."

A challenge? He enjoyed those and when they involved carnal activities with Julia, all the better. "Oh, I intend to."

Damn it, had this hallway always been so long? Reaching his chambers, after what seemed like forever, he shouldered his way into the room, kicking the door shut behind him. After setting Julia down, he began to disrobe, tearing off his cravat, followed by his boots. "Can you get that off on your own?" he asked, nodding to her dress.

"Yes," she replied. "Anxious, are we?"

Hell yes, he was. It didn't matter that this wasn't his idea, he was committed now. "Not anxious. Efficient."

"I like efficiency." She began to peel off her gown, which distracted him from his own task of disrobing. He paused with one boot in his hand, the other still on his foot, and watched her creamy skin appear, inch by delicious inch. "Sebastian, you've lost your efficiency," she teased when she caught him staring.

"Right, so I have." Sitting on the bed he tugged off his remaining shoe. "My apologies."

Once they were both naked, he pulled her into his arms and lifted her onto the bed. Their kisses began slow and gentle; Sebastian took his time exploring her mouth, the slightly salty column of her throat, the sensitive spot behind her ear. She was every bit as intoxicating now as she had been the first time in his bed, and somehow he knew she always would be. He sounded like a sodding madman, but to hell with it.

His attention drifted to her breasts. Her skin was soft and smooth, pearly white in the soft candlelight.

"Tell me again," she moaned, fingers sifting through his hair.

"What?" His palms slid over her stomach.

"You know what."

He smiled and kissed one rosy nipple, then the other. "I love you."

"Again, please."

"Please?" he laughed.

"I may be demanding, but I'm also polite."

Sebastian's hands moved lower, stroking her thighs. "Yes, you are. And I love you."

Her moans enticed him, ratcheting up his excitement. As much as he enjoyed the anticipation, he needed her, and soon. "Sebastian …"

"More demands?" One finger slipped inside her tight heat and he groaned.

"One." Her hand brushed against his erection, and stroked with a clumsy but effective rhythm. "Need you …"

Thank the bloody heavens. Slow and steady wasn't something he found particularly appealing at the moment. "We'll go slow next time, sweetheart," he murmured against her ear as he guided himself to her entrance. Perfection.

With one fluid thrust he hilted and immediately began to move; swift, deep strokes that made his senses reel. Her hips rose and fell in time with his, creating a wonderful friction and the sense of completion overwhelmed him.

Julia's tiny, mewling cries grew louder, her movements more frantic, and when he felt the fluttering that signaled her climax, he clenched his jaw, grinding his teeth in an effort to hold his own orgasm at bay. Then he caught sight of her face —eyes squeezed, mouth open in a silent scream. God, she was beautiful. With one final thrust, he went still and surrendered. Sebastian pressed a kiss to her forehead and rolled onto his back, pulling her with him so that she settled against his side. "In case you wish to hear it again," he panted, "and even if you don't—I love you."

•

"Marry me," Sebastian said some time later. She was cradled against his chest, about to drift to sleep.

"What?" Pushing herself up she leaned on one elbow and blinked at him.

"Marry me."

"Is that a proposal?" she asked.

He grinned. "I was going to ask you tomorrow. But since you're here, yes. I want you as my wife, my duchess, and the mother of my children. Will you marry me?"

She blinked again. Had she fallen asleep? Was she dreaming? "What will we do about Thomas?"

"Tomorrow I will take the journal to Amelia's father. I imagine he will want to deal with Suffolk himself. If not, I don't care about rumors; let him say what he wants. Now, are you going to answer me or must I ask again?"

"Yes," Julia replied with a smile. It didn't require much thought. She'd wanted nothing more than to hear those words for weeks. "Yes, I will marry you."

Sebastian kissed her soundly. "Good. I suspect my solicitor is still up working on the special license I requested. I'd hate to think the poor man lost sleep for nothing."

"You want to rush the wedding?" It was probably a good idea, but she hadn't considered it. Still, she didn't care about a big fancy ceremony, or any of that society nonsense.

"Well, no, we don't have to. Call it my being overeager. We'll do whatever you want, sweetheart."

What was wrong with being eager? "Let's not wait," she told him, leaning in for another kiss. "The sooner you can call me your wife, the happier I'll be."

"That, my love, makes two of us."

Chapter Fifteen

*T*he Marquis of Landsdowne looked up from the last page of his daughter's diary. The trio was seated in the Marquis' parlor, three cups of tea slowly going cold, ignored on the table. Julia had requested she come along, and against his better judgment, Sebastian had agreed. In truth, he hadn't expected Amelia's father to see him. "Where did you get this, Rutland?"

His expression was pained, voice tinged with anguish over reopened wounds that had clearly never healed.

Sebastian paused. He wasn't sure it would be wise to tell the truth. If anything, let Landsdowne think it had been he who rifled through Suffolk's private study and stole the journal.

"I took it from Thomas's study," Julia said.

So much for that idea.

"What were you doing in Suffolk's study, Miss Deveraux?"

She shrugged. "Prying."

Landsdowne held up a hand. "I'm not sure I want to know."

"My father sought to force a marriage to Lord Suffolk. Your daughter may have saved my life, my lord."

The Marquis looked close to tears. Removing his spectacles he wiped at his eyes. "I had no idea she was seeing Suffolk. He'd shown an interest in her, and I wasn't pleased, but I thought she had rebuked his advances. She told me you cried off, but never said why. Rutland, had I known—"

Sebastian fought his own tears. Julia's flowed freely. "I know," he replied. "I've spent five years hating myself."

"I tried to hate you, but it was clear you punished yourself more than I could have, so I left you alone."

"Will you go to the authorities?" Julia asked.

Landsdowne sighed and shook his head. "I don't know. I doubt they will think this enough evidence to accuse an earl of murder."

Sebastian had to agree. "You could hire a Runner. I don't know what they would be able to turn up after all this time, but it's worth a try. I will pay for it."

"No need, Rutland. You've paid enough." His eyes flicked to Julia. "Are you and Miss Deveraux—"

"We are."

"Ironic, isn't it?" Landsdowne mused.

It was that, to be sure. "Fate is not without a sense of—"

"Justice," the older man supplied. "It's alright, you know."

"What is?"

"To take revenge by being happy."

"No," Sebastian said, "I have no interest in revenge anymore." His gaze darted once again to his fiancée, who was studying her hands with interest. His mother's ring sparkled on her finger, a flash of rubies and diamonds. After all the work he'd done to secure her affections, he couldn't let the Marquis put doubt back into her mind.

"Rutland, my father used to tell me that the best revenge against your enemies is to live well. So live well with Miss Deveraux, and if you find satisfaction in the fact that you are happy, and Suffolk is not, what's wrong with that?"

"Nothing," Julia answered, and smiled. "Nothing that I can see."

Now that was interesting. But, inconsequential, because for the first time he could say with absolute honesty that revenge was not what he desired. "I don't care about revenge anymore," he said. "Now that it's within reach, I simply don't care."

Landsdowne nodded. "That, your Grace, is what makes it alright."

•

"So what now?" Julia asked. She was seated next to Sebastian in his carriage on the way to her father's townhome. The Marquis was on his way to speak with the authorities, journal in hand. He'd promised to send word as soon as he knew something.

"We speak with your father about our engagement." Sebastian had been quiet all morning, and Julia understood that he had a great deal on his mind, so she tried to give him his space, but heavens, there had been some drastic changes for her as well. She was engaged, in love, and loved in return! Who could she tell? Her father to start with, yes, then Aunt Margaret, but she wanted everyone to know. It sounded ridiculous, but it was true.

The Viscount was not in his study when they arrived at the townhome, but Thomas Howard was. Seated behind the large desk, he looked up from the stack of papers in his hands when they entered. "Ah, good. I was hoping it would be the both of you," he said and stood.

"What are you doing?" Julia asked. "Rifling through my father's papers?"

Thomas grinned. "Tit for tat, my dear. You may be the only female in England who doesn't keep a journal, and since there was nothing of interest in your private things, I decided to search your father's. I have found some intriguing secrets here. Would you like to hear them?"

"What are you talking about, Thomas?"

"Don't be angry with Edwards, dove. He only told me after I broke two of his fingers." For emphasis, he held up one hand and wiggled his own fingers. "But he did, eventually, tell me you'd been alone in my study. So where is it?"

She looked to Sebastian. He was standing immobile in the doorway, shoulders rigid. "I don't know what you're talking about," she lied.

"I think you do, princess." He took a step forward and nodded to her hand. "Nice ring. I think, though, that it must be on the wrong finger, since I did not give it to you."

"It's where it should be," Sebastian spoke for the first time.

"She's engaged to me, Rutland."

"Actually, she's not."

"No? Then why in the hell did I pay off the debts of her worthless idiot father?"

Julia's hands clenched. "One worthless idiot helping another, I suppose?"

Reaching into his overcoat, Thomas withdrew a pistol and trained it on her. "I'd advise you not say anything like that again." Sebastian took a step forward, and Thomas swung the weapon in his direction. "Not another step, Rutland."

"She doesn't have the bloody journal."

"I'll take it off your hands, then."

"I don't have it either," he stated. "You'll have to find the Marquis of Landsdowne and have him get it back from the authorities if you want it so badly."

Suffolk paled. For the first time, his icy veneer started to crack, and a bead of sweat rolled down his forehead. "You're lying. Landsdowne wouldn't sully the reputation of his dead daughter by showing the world what a whore she was."

It was difficult to think with a weapon being pointed alternately at her and the man she loved, but Julia tried to focus. She could see Sebastian's body was tense, knew he was watching for the right time to strike. His expression was one of blank calm, but the way he shifted his weight forward and the subtle movements of his hands told her he was formulating a plan. If she could distract Thomas, perhaps Sebastian could get the gun.

"Where is my aunt?" Julia asked.

The pistol swiveled back to her. "That deaf old witch is sound asleep upstairs. I checked when I first got here."

"There's no need to be insulting, Thomas."

"Take that ring off, then tell me where the journal really is, and perhaps I'll be more inclined to compromise."

"Why did you kill her?" she asked, changing tactics.

"I don't recall saying I did."

Julia raised an eyebrow. "Then how did you come by her diary? And why have you been hiding it for five years? Did you ever love her?"

His laugh was harsh and grating. There was a cruel glint in his eyes that answered the question before he spoke. "I've never loved anyone. She was decent enough in bed and the knowledge that bedding her would damage your tortured hero was enough satisfaction for me. I imagine I would have married her, had her father not been the Marquis of Landsdowne. He's powerful, rich, and nothing could be done to quell him, unlike your own pathetic father."

Thomas had taken another step forward as he spoke. Out of the corner of her eye she saw Sebastian give an almost imperceptible nod. A few more steps, and Thomas would have nearly turned his back. Julia took a breath and started talking again.

"So that's why you chose me? My father?"

"At first, yes. You're pretty enough, of course, but I thought you would be docile, having lived your life in the country. Henry is as close to destitute as I've seen, easily controlled. When you took off dressed like a bloody man, you proved to be feistier than I'd anticipated," another step, "and I nearly called it off." Another. "Then I learned where you were." Two more steps. Almost… "I found the urge to torture my old friend irresistible. I suppose you could say I enjoy being cruel."

He took one more step and Sebastian lunged forward. Crouched low, his considerable bulk slammed into Thomas's side, and the force of the blow sent them both crashing to the floor. Thomas howled; the pistol flew from his hands and skittered across the floor under the desk. Sebastian seemed to have the upper hand, at least for now. His fist connected with Thomas's face, and she heard the sickening crunch of breaking bone.

Thomas retaliated with a blow of his own. Sebastian's head snapped back from a punch to his jaw, and his grip loosened for a brief moment. It was long enough to allow Thomas the chance to push him away and stand.

"I've been waiting five years for a rematch, Rutland," Thomas growled. Blood leaked from his nose, creating a crimson trail down his chin and bloomed on the white cloth of his cravat.

Julia looked from the desk to the two men. They were more or less evenly matched, and both looked equally determined to kill the other. She needed to get that gun. Keeping her eyes trained on the fight, she slid along the wall until facing the desk. The barrel of the gun was peeking out from beneath the desk, and Julia breathed a sigh of relief as she bent to retrieve it. It was heavy and cold in her hand. Deadly. She shivered.

Okay, now what? Raising the gun, she shouted, "Stop!"

Both men turned. Sebastian gaped at her. It seemed he expected her to shoot herself by accident. Pity she didn't have more confidence.

Thomas laughed. "I'm to believe you know how to use a gun?"

He was, unfortunately, correct. She didn't know the first thing about firing a pistol. Even if she did, the men were too close together, and moving too rapidly for her to risk it. Taking advantage of the distraction, Sebastian landed a successful punch to the right side of Thomas's face, sending a fine spray of blood across the carpet.

"Go ahead and shoot me, princess," he shouted, fist lashing out at Sebastian's midsection. "With any luck you'll catch Rutland in the head."

She couldn't do it, and he knew that. Alright, time for a new plan. She couldn't let them pummel each other to death.

Aunt Margaret's form appeared in the doorway, the small cat figurine from the foyer in her hands. She winked at Julia, and crept over to the struggling gentlemen.

The statuette shattered as it hit Thomas's head with a sharp crack.

"That's for calling me a deaf old witch, you bloody bastard," Margaret said.

Thomas reached for the back of his head with one hand. Wide eyes, full of shock, shifted from Julia to Sebastian and back again. "What the—" Without finesse, he slumped to the ground.

"I was on the verge of besting him, I'll have you know," Sebastian said, looking somewhat sullen for having been robbed of victory.

"I know, dear," Margaret replied. "But it was highly satisfying. Been wanting to hit that clod pole for weeks now."

"I've waited years, my lady."

"Well," she sat on the couch and waved her hands, "you got more than a few good licks in, your Grace. I'd say you thoroughly rearranged his face, in fact. It's almost a pity, that countenance was the only thing about him not completely loathsome. Now he's ugly inside and out."

"I'll send my footman for the authorities," Sebastian announced.

"No need," Margaret replied. "I sent Anders already, he should be back soon."

Julia felt a rush of relief. "Should we tie him up?"

"I doubt that's necessary," Sebastian said, limping over to her, "but I'd like for you to give me the gun, sweetheart."

She relinquished the weapon. "Ugh, take it, please."

"Are you alright?" His hands skimmed down her sides, then cupped her face as he inspected her for injury.

"I'm fine, Sebastian. You're bleeding." There was a cut below his right eye, and blood dripped from his lower lip.

"I'm fine, sweetheart. It's nothing." Pulling her into his arms he held her tight. "It's over. We're free."

"So," Aunt Margaret piped up, "Does this mean happily ever after?"

Sebastian's chuckle rumbled against her ear, low and comforting. "I believe it does."

Chapter Sixteen

"**W**elcome home, your Graces." Mrs. Holland, Elizabeth, William, and the rest of Foxwaith's staff were lined up along the entrance to the estate as Sebastian stepped over the threshold of his family home for the first time as a married man. The woman at his side looked a bit overwhelmed. They'd been married for three days, but Julia still hadn't adjusted to being the Duchess of Rutland. She had, however, adjusted very well to being his wife, which was most important to him.

Julia's father had started asking for money within minutes of learning about the engagement. Sebastian had been inclined to give it to him, but Julia stopped him. So he'd struck a bargain with Hereford; the man received a monthly allowance, but if he exceeded it, he would repay every last farthing by working on one of Sebastian's cargo ships—in America.

Thomas Howard, Earl of Suffolk, was currently awaiting trial in Newgate. While the journal alone was not enough to convince the authorities that he had murdered Amelia, Julia and Sebastian's statements had given them the added proof they required.

"This is acceptable," Lady Margaret said, stepping in behind them. She had accepted their invitation to live at Foxwaith without hesitation, but had wanted to come later, after the newlyweds had spent time alone. Julia insisted she come immediately.

"I'm glad you like it, Aunt," Julia replied. Introductions were made, and Mrs. Holland led Margaret up to her new room to help her get settled.

"I'll see to your bags, milady," Elizabeth announced. "If ye need me, I'll be in yer rooms unpackin'."

"Thank you, Elizabeth. I'm sure I'll be fine," Julia smiled, holding tight to Sebastian's arm.

"Yes, Elizabeth, she'll be fine," he repeated. "Just don't try the connecting door to my rooms. I believe we'll be occupied for a bit."

"Sebastian!"

His wife—*wife*! he thought wildly, flushed, and gave her arm a tug. He grinned. "Well, it was just a suggestion. Do you have a better idea, wife?"

"As a matter of fact, husband, I don't."

She squealed when he swept her into his arms and started up the stairs. Their servants were staring, and truth be told, he didn't care. He was married. He was in love. There was nothing wrong with those around him knowing.

He set Julia down once they'd reached his chambers. "Alex has requested that I lock us in here and not leave until we make a baby."

She lifted an eyebrow and smiled. "Did he? Since when do you take orders from your brother?"

Sebastian loosened his cravat. "On the rare occasion he has an exceedingly good idea."

"Ah." She stepped into his arms and offered her lips for a kiss. "Is it, perhaps, the activity leading to conception that you find so appealing?"

"Naturally." He kissed her. "I love you, Julia."

"And I love you."

She'd been more than his revenge, more than his second chance. She was his redemption.

• • •

Kayleigh Jamison

A writer and musician at an early age, Kayleigh Jamison wrote her first novella at the age of seven, and first picked up a violin at eight. By eighteen, she had won several state and regional awards for the performing arts. With a Bachelors degree in English and Philosophy and a Certification in Legal Studies, Kayleigh is currently a full-time third-year law student by day and renegade romance writer by night. She enjoys rewriting history, exploring not only what was, but what could have been, mixing real historical figures and events with spicy, no-holds-barred fiction.

"I'm not so much a creator," she often says of her work, "as I am a medium. I channel something greater than myself, and bring these stories to life in ways that surprise even me."

Kayleigh is a member of RWA and her local chapter First Coast Romance Writers, the Historical Romance Society, and the Historical Novel Society. She currently lives in northern Florida, just miles from the Atlantic, with her two cats, Angel and Jackson, and a rescue rat named Schmuckers.

www.KayleighJamison.com